Also by Kate Parker

The Deadly Series
Deadly Scandal
Deadly Wedding
Deadly Fashion
Deadly Deception

The Victorian Bookshop Mysteries
The Vanishing Thief
The Counterfeit Lady
The Royal Assassin
The Conspiring Woman
The Detecting Duchess

The Milliner Mysteries
The Killing at Kaldaire House

The Mystery at Chadwick House

Kate Parker

JDP Press

ISBN: 978-0-9976637-2-3 [e-book]

ISBN: 978-0-9976637-3-0 [print]

Published by JDP Press

Cover design by Kim Killion of The Killion Group, Inc.

Dedication

To my many friends in New Bern, who made my life there wonderful, and who have had to go through so much since the hurricane.

Chapter One

The largest bedroom in Bev's once-elegant Victorian fixer-upper was massive, with a wide plank floor and ornate trim work on the ceiling and around the windows. The windows provided a terrific view of the street framed by the branches of the two stately oak trees in the front yard. I walked around the empty iron bedstead and a chest of drawers leaning on two legs to look out the closest window as Bev discussed navy blue and cornflower for the decor.

I was a foot away from the window ledge when I first felt a crushing pain gripping my chest; then my airway began to close. I tried to speak, but no sound came out as the pain and lack of oxygen blurred my vision. I retreated to the hallway, gasping for breath.

"Emma. What's wrong?" When I could focus, I found myself leaning on the top of the banister with Bev staring into my face, one hand on my arm.

"I don't know. The dust in there, or the heat. Something made it hard to breathe. Your new house is wonderful, Bev, but I've got to get out of here. Let me go outside and snap some 'before' pictures while I get some air."

I bolted down the stairs and out the front door like I was being chased. Once beyond the overgrown bushes and the missing step to the front porch, the tension in my chest relaxed, but my heart was still beating too fast and I was breathing hard. It wasn't dust. It wasn't heat. I'd never reacted to either this way before. And I wasn't ill. Two deep breaths and I was fine now that I was out of the house. I didn't know what the problem was, but I never wanted to experience it again.

Pulling out my camera, I walked to the street and turned around to take a picture of Bev on her new front porch.

"Not with me in it, silly," she yelled and went back into the house.

I walked into the yard of the Fenster-Willoughby House next door, an elegant antebellum owned by a renowned cellist, to take a picture at an angle, and then walked into Walnut Street to get the entire front of Bev's newly purchased dream house in my camera frame. I'd taken two shots when a horn blew and I turned to see a mammoth Buick rumbling toward me.

The horn shocked me for an instant. The car was nearly on top of me before I could think to jump backwards out of the way. An octogenarian looked straight ahead through the steering wheel as she barreled past without slowing.

"That woman's a menace."

I swung around at the sound of the nice baritone to

find a man next to me in one of the yards across from Bev's house. He looked as nice as he sounded. A couple of inches taller than me in the sandals I was wearing, he had a wiry build and wore a collarless shirt and work pants in a rough material. It was his smile, though, as he stood leaning against a tree, that drew me closer.

He must have been working in his yard and watched my near demise. Staring at him, I couldn't remember the names of anyone who lived in these turn-of-the-century houses, "workers' houses," on narrow lots across from the spacious Chadwick and Fenster-Willoughby houses. It also took me a moment to remember how to speak. "Does she do that often?" I finally stammered.

"All the time." The man belatedly looked concerned. "Are you all right?"

"I'm fine. I'm Emma Winter." I finally thought to introduce myself.

"Adam Chadwick." He had a ready smile and beautiful eyes. I've always been a sucker for beautiful eyes. "Did you buy the old homestead?"

"No. My friends Bev and Roger did. Is the Chadwick house your family home?"

He shook his head and a lock of pale brown hair fell almost to his long-lashed blue eyes. "There are a lot of Chadwicks around here."

Why is it only guys have long gorgeous lashes? "I thought like a lot of old families, they've almost died out."

"There're a few of us lingering on."

We exchanged smiles and fell into an awkward silence. Finally, I said, "Let me get a couple more photos and I'll introduce you to your new neighbor."

I stepped back into the street and lined up my shot. As soon as I clicked the shutter, Bev came out the door and walked toward me. "Ready to go?"

"I want to introduce you to—" I turned back to the yard across the street, but the man had disappeared. "Oh, never mind. He's gone now."

"Who?"

"Adam Chadwick. He was right there under that tree."

"Chadwick? Like my house?"

"Yeah. He said there's a few of them about."

Bev looked perplexed. "The lawyers said there aren't any left."

"Not that part of the family, but I'm sure there are third cousins or something here in Summerduck."

She shrugged. "Have enough shots? I'm hungry."

"One more. There. Let's eat." I put my camera in my bag and we walked toward downtown and a riverside restaurant.

After we ate, I walked home to my apartment on the second floor of a house built in the twenties. Flipping on my computer, I put in the camera card and looked at the shots I'd taken. My plan was to print off my shots of the house, or rather, the ones in focus that didn't cut off the roof or the front porch. I studied them for a minute, trying to decide which shot was best, when I noticed something in a front upstairs window.

Bev had gone back into the house. It would make a cute picture if that was her looking out the window and not a shadow or a smudge on my lens.

I looked harder. There it was in two more pictures. Out of curiosity, I blew up all three. If I squinted, there was definitely a face in the window. But it wasn't Bev. This was a man, and he had a mustache.

Had he been there all the time we'd been in the house? Who was he? A tramp hiding in the attic of the empty house? I needed to let Bev and Roger know they had a squatter.

I jogged to the house they rented a few streets over from their new home and ran to the door clutching the photos. When I pounded on the door, Bev answered with, "I thought Roger had forgotten his keys again." Then she looked at my face and said, "What's happened?"

"Look at these." I shoved the enlargements at her.

"Oh, they turned out well. Come in. I have to stir dinner or it'll burn." She walked into the house carrying my photos.

"Look at the upstairs windows."

She stirred delicious-smelling sautéing vegetables and then peered at the photos. "It looks like a face."

I breathed deeply over her dinner and then sighed. Bev was a fabulous cook. "It is a face. Someone was in your house today."

She set down her spoon and studied the pictures. "But we didn't see anyone."

"We wouldn't if he's living in this empty house and stayed in hiding."

Bev looked angry. "You mean our new house came with a tenant?"

"More like a squatter. You need to have someone check out the entire house for you and then change the locks."

"Changing the locks sounds good. Hello, hon." Roger Myers, surgeon and Bev's husband, came in around me to give his wife a kiss. "Hey, Emma." Then he completely ignored me as he said, "Dinner smells good. We'll have to eat fast. I'm on call tonight."

I was relieved to see his scrubs were clean. I've always been squeamish about gore. "Hey, Roger. You've got a lodger in your new house."

"What?" He grabbed the photos his wife held out. "What are you talking about?"

"See the face in the upstairs window?"

"No."

"It's hard to make out, but it's there," Bev said.

"There's a smudge in that window, but I don't think it's a face. Defect in the old glass, maybe."

"It's a face." I was sure.

He shook his head, set the photos down, and leaned over the stove as he picked up a fork.

"I'll dish up dinner," Bev said. "Thanks for bringing the photos by, Em. It can't hurt to have someone check out the house and change the locks."

"Yes. Good plan. Now, I am famished. Let's eat," Roger said.

I knew it was my cue to leave. I glanced at the stove while Bev dished up something with tomatoes and zucchini and then showed myself out.

I walked the few blocks home, where I recognized the tall bulk of police Sergeant Mike Randall on the front porch. One-hundred percent brave, never backs down, cool, professional, but totally sexist jackass, and childhood friend, Mike Randall. Bev says he has pretty blue eyes, but I could never get past his raunchy tongue.

Mike was the nephew of the Summerduck fire chief, Bobby Aster, my downstairs neighbor and landlord. Bobby's wife was my Aunt Jean, which was how I ended up living in their upstairs apartment.

Two men couldn't have been more different. Bobby was a southern gentleman. Mike could have been trailer trash if the mobile home parks lowered their standards.

Mike looked up before I could find a way to escape, and I found myself staring into the face of a man who'd never understood a clean joke. I'm sure the eyes hiding behind the mirrored sunglasses were grinning as much as his smirking mouth.

As long as I was cornered, I had an idea. "Are you working tomorrow?"

One eyebrow arched over the sunglasses. "I start at noon. What you got in mind, Sugarbear?"

I could tell what he had in mind. Bev, Mike, and I had gone the whole way through school together. Bev was my BFF. Mike was the friend I had a secret crush on until junior high school, when he decided to take after his no-account daddy and not his kind, sensible Uncle Bobby. "Could you meet me at the Chadwick house tomorrow when you come on duty? There might be a squatter living there."

His expression changed to all business, thin-lipped and square-jawed. If he weren't such a jerk, leering at me while I walked up stairs, we'd still be good friends.

"Bev and Roger Myers just bought the place. I was taking pictures and caught a man looking out a window at us."

"We'll need permission of the new owners."

"I'll bring Bev."

He nodded and walked off to his squad car.

Bev agreed to meet me at lunchtime at her new house and brought a locksmith and the photos with her. Mike showed up on time and in uniform. Once Bev unlocked the door, he ordered us to wait on the porch while he went in.

We left the front door open and listened to his footsteps boom over the first floor of the nearly empty house and echo up the stairs. Then Bev and I stuck our heads inside in unison and listened while something heavy pounded around the upstairs and then clomped up to the attic. The locksmith stayed in his white van.

"I see you asked Sergeant Randall to check out the house for us." Bev gave me a knowing smile. She'd been trying to fix me up with Mike since my jackass ex left me. She didn't understand that while Mike wasn't so bad as a friend, I didn't want to trade an indiscriminate prick for a sexist pig. Bev wouldn't let it go. She thought we looked good together.

"He was on the front porch when I came home from your place. I had to think of something to say to him."

"How sweet," she said, not paying any attention to me as she stepped into the foyer of the house and gazed up the stairs. My gaze was drawn there as well to the beautiful stained-glass window halfway up the staircase.

When Randall finally returned, shoving his flashlight back into place on his belt, he said, "What made you think there was anyone in here?"

"These photos," Bev said, showing him my work.

He looked from the photos to Bev. "So?"

"Don't you see the face in the upstairs window?"

"A trick of the lighting. Old glass. Whatever, there's no sign of anyone hiding or living in here."

"Are you sure?" I asked.

"Yes. Just a lot of junk to clear out. Get the locks changed or whatever makes you feel safer, but there's no reason for the police to be involved."

Bev walked past us into the living room and Randall leaned toward me. In a low voice he said, "Any place else you've been seeing ghosts, honeybear?"

"No. Thank. You. Sergeant."

"Good day, ladies," he said with a smirk as he marched off to his car. I watched his blue-clad toned rear end and muscular thighs walk away. I suspected I wasn't the only one in town who'd think "tight sphincter." Still, it was a nice view.

The young Burmese locksmith walked past me carrying his toolbox. He entered the house calling "Miz Myers," as Randall drove off. I was about to follow the locksmith when I spotted Adam Chadwick. I waved and he crossed the street to join me on the front lawn.

"You haven't seen anyone hanging around this house lately, have you?"

His warm smile disappeared into a frown. "No one's lived here since old man Duffy died. Of course, you've been hanging around lately." He smiled again. "I rather like that."

"When I was taking pictures yesterday, I caught a man looking from an upstairs window at us."

"That old glass can reflect all sorts of images." He didn't exactly scoff at my words, but he didn't agree, either.

Like Roger. Like Mike Randall. What was it with men? "He was in three of the photos. And he had a mustache. That much is clear."

He shook his head. "Which window was it?"

"The far right. In the master bedroom." I glanced back at the window. And blinked. "He's there again."

Adam's voice took on an angry tone as he said, "And your friend's in there with him? Union soldiers."

Chapter Two

"You think that's a Union soldier in there?" I eyed Adam cautiously. He was nice to look at but he made no sense.

"An old expression used around here since the—," Adam Chadwick smiled, "War of Northern Aggression. I used to hear my grandfather say that whenever anything was wrong. Better than cussing."

"We just had the house checked out by the police. No one was inside. Where did he come from?"

"Emma, it's an old house. There could be hidden passages, ghosts, all sorts of secrets. I just hope your friend doesn't discover that house isn't what she wanted. It's a nice old house. Deserves a nice family."

"Bev loves that house. She's been over every inch of it. Why should it not be what she wants?" I felt a need to defend Bev and the house, but I had no idea why. I looked up at the window again. The man's face was still visible.

Working on a theory, I moved closer to the house with my eyes fixed on the second-story window. It was definitely a man's face, but I was seeing him from a different angle. If the vision had been a reflection in warped glass, I'd now be seeing a totally different reflection. Trees or swirls or bunny rabbits.

Adam remained in place, glaring up at the window. The man in the window stared back at him. My imagination must have been running away with me, because I thought I could see hatred on both their faces.

Leaving them to their staring contest, I hurried inside and rushed up the stairs as quietly as I could. Then I found I didn't want to take the last few steps along the landing to the open door of the master bedroom. Cold air smelling of dust and rot surrounded me.

I forced myself to take those last steps and peeked around the edge of the door frame. For an instant, I thought I saw a man standing with his back to me at the window. Then there was nothing. Just an empty room and my wild imagination. I didn't see any footprints in the dust, smell aftershave, or hear squeaking floorboards.

I went back downstairs slowly, wondering if I were crazy. At the bottom, I looked out to where Adam had been. He was gone.

* * *

At first, Bev was ecstatic about how quickly the workmen were clearing out the underbrush in the yard and the vines off the walls. Of course, a cleaned-up yard showed a lack of grass as well as the dismal state of the house and the large garage in the backyard. Chipped paint, rotted boards, and cracked windows were just the most obvious signs of decay.

Since Roger always seemed to be at the hospital or

having office hours, Bev appointed me her "muscle" in dealing with contractors. We laughed about her description for my role, since I've always been thin.

However, Bev decided if you can't have a male present to convince brawny craftsmen to do what you want, an actress from the local theater who can spout legal-sounding nonsense about contracts and building codes might frighten them into submission. The fact she was paying me went a long way to ensure I'd be available for whatever role whenever she needed.

When I had found out about my ex cheating on me with half the women in town, I flipped out for a while. Bev was there to visit me in the hospital, hold my hand, listen to my sobs, and mend broken fences when I'd taken my hurt and anger and revenge too far. No one has ever accused me of being calm and sensible even on my good days. I owed her a lot.

And spending time at Bev's new house meant a chance to see Adam again. I asked a few friends, checked the phone book and local land records, but I couldn't find a trace of him. He didn't live across the street, but he didn't seem homeless.

He didn't act or smell like the homeless we have living in the swamps and farmland of eastern North Carolina. Living on casual labor or VA disability, bunking in a dilapidated singlewide trailer with a friend or a cousin.

Adam was clean, for one thing, and neatly groomed. He was cleanshaven. He showed no signs of addiction or mental illness. I hadn't checked to see whether he could read, but he seemed educated, and there was no visible physical injury that would explain disability payments from the VA.

There must be a reason why Adam wasn't known around Summerduck and I was determined to uncover that reason. All I needed was time.

When Bev next called me from her cellphone at the Chadwick place, she sounded desperate. Now able to walk around the outside of the house without needing a machete to clear a trail, I hurried from the front sidewalk toward the sounds of voices. I found Bev in the backyard talking to two men in jeans, work boots, and polo shirts, and one little old lady in a starched cotton dress and rain boots. Actually, the little old lady with the helmet of pinkish white hair and pearls was doing all of the talking.

"That barn is a historic structure and you cannot tear it down. This is a historic district and the Historical Society will not allow it."

"You have a barn?" I asked Bev quietly.

She pointed at the garage.

At least that explained why there was a two-car garage in the backyard and no way to drive to it before the bushes were hacked away. I had to ask. "Why is the barn historic?"

Bev glared at me.

"Who are you?" the woman with the pinkish white hair asked.

"Emma Winter. And you?" I also wanted to ask why she was wearing pearls with her red rubber boots but decided that would be a step too far.

"Doris Carmichael, chairwoman of the Historical Society."

"So why—?"

"Because this is the site of the famous Chadwick murders."

"There was a murder in my house?" Bev demanded, not looking like she was happy about where this conversation was heading.

"No, not in the house. In the barn. Although one of the combatants lingered for over a week, dying in the house."

As the woman turned to say something to one of the men, who I now noticed wore a shirt with the city logo, I said, "What happened?"

"Two brothers got into a fight in the barn. Both were stabbed. When people came in response to their sister's screams, they found one dead. The live brother claimed the dead brother had started the fight, and there were no witnesses to say otherwise. On the day of the funeral, the living brother fell ill with lockjaw, and he died a few days later. Apparently, his wound was infected since the stabbing took place in the barn. The barn has since been declared a historic building."

A story like that would lead the local news for a few days. "When did this happen?"

"1904."

I made a face like I'd tasted something foul. "And nothing's been done to the barn since then."

The old woman glared at me. "It was used as a shed after people stopped keeping animals within historic district limits. Probably still has antique farm implements inside."

We walked over as a group and the two men donned work gloves to yank on the rotted wooden door at one end. It splintered and one of the boards fell off, but they managed to open a space a few feet wide. A bird flew out, making us all jump. Inside weeds grew in clumps on the dirt floor and rusted iron tools hung from nails. My nose twitched as I checked my shoes. The man who I guessed was the painter I was supposed to meet that day pointed to the ground just inside the doorway. "Historic animal poop."

A dark look from the old woman stopped me in mid-snicker. I looked into the barn to find out how the less-than-historic animal had pooped in a closed building. I could see daylight where a few boards were missing from the door at the far side of the structure. Then I looked up. Half the roof was missing. "If you can be patient through the winter, this barn will have collapsed by next spring."

"No. I won't allow it. You'll have to repair this building." Mrs. Carmichael was adamant. Her jowls and her pearls shook, but her permed and sprayed helmet of hair didn't move.

"No efforts were made to have this structure repaired before now. A good case could be made for arbitrary implementation by the Historical Society if they try to enforce action at such a late date. Good thing I've got my camera." I pulled it out of my canvas bag and began to shoot pictures, showing the worst of the damage and rot.

The city worker, who I now suspected was an inspector, leafed through some papers. "I don't see any Historical Society filings on this building in the last ten years. I'd think the neighbors would be glad to see it go."

"That's not the point. Historical structures should be maintained." Mrs. Carmichael turned to Bev. "You bought this house subject to historical covenants."

"Yes, but—" Bev looked extremely uncomfortable as I guessed she saw the bills to renovate the house skyrocket.

"Why didn't the Historical Society pursue this with the previous owner?" I asked.

"Mr. Duffy was descended from the Chadwicks," Mrs. Carmichael answered as if this explained everything.

"So? He was the previous owner, who allowed this structure to become so dilapidated it cannot be repaired. Why did the Historical Society allow that?" I asked, eyebrows raised.

The painter backed away and said, "I've got to get going."

Bev said, "Let's take a quick look at the outside of the house so you can give me an estimate."

They walked off, leaving me with an uneasy city inspector and a rabid historical preservationist.

"I'm going to bring this up to the committee. You won't get away with this," Mrs. Carmichael said as her parting shot, stomping away in her red rubber boots.

I looked at the inspector. He smiled and said, "Have a blessed day," before he left, going around the far side of the house from Mrs. Carmichael.

I suspected he'd dealt with her before.

I took a few more shots of the shack, as I was beginning to think of it. When I turned around, I nearly bumped into Adam Chadwick.

"Oh, hello." My pulse rate rose. I so seldom met nice guys my age who didn't avoid me because of my psychiatric history. No, it was more than that. If he did know my life story, he didn't bring it up. If he didn't, I wasn't about to tell him. He had the gentlest blue eyes that always seemed to smile at me.

"Hello." He looked past me at the barn. "Now that the vines are off of it, that old place is looking sad. Have you been inside?"

"No, thank you. It looks like a strong breeze would knock it down."

He moved past me and set one foot inside. "Oh, look at those old tillers and hoes. Left to rust and decay. Nothing here but junk. Old Duffy let things fall apart in his last years. Of course, I don't think he was quite right, as they say."

"You knew him?" I asked as he stepped away from the barn.

"He used to come outside and we'd talk. The last few years, he seldom did even that."

Whoever Adam was, he wasn't a transient. I noticed his clothes looked the same as they had when we first met. He must frequently launder them, because they looked fresh and there was no smell of sweat despite the heat. "So, you live around here?"

"Yes. Your friend seems to be doing the old house a lot of good. Things Duffy hadn't seen to in years."

"Did you ask him why?"

He shrugged. "No money. No energy. No interest. He seemed to be slowly dying for years, ever since his mother passed away."

"You knew his mother?"

"As an old, old woman. She lived to be almost one hundred."

"Amazing. Say, would you like to meet for a cup of coffee sometime? You could tell me the story behind this house."

He looked surprised, and then smiled. "Yes, I'd like that, Emma. Where shall we meet?"

"Tonight at Carolina Coffee?"

"Sounds good. What time?"

"Eight o'clock?" Everything in the historic downtown area closed at nine, even in the summer. And on a weeknight, there'd be few people out at eight.

"And after coffee, maybe we can go for a stroll." His smile widened.

None of my alarm bells were going off about this guy, but then, none had gone off about my ex, either. Oh, why not, I decided. It's only coffee. "I'd like that. Eight isn't too late for you for caffeine?"

"I don't sleep much, but if you would rather not—"

"Oh. No. I'll get decaf." I gave him a reassuring smile and hoped I didn't sound desperate. "Why don't you sleep much?"

He shrugged, giving me a better view of broad

shoulders as the fabric slid across his chest. "Too restless, I guess. There's always something else to see and do."

"You don't strike me as the ambitious sort."

"I was, once. Now I try to be curious about the world around me without wanting to have everything I see. How about you? Are you ambitious?"

"No. That's why I'm an artist and actress in Summerduck and not New York."

We exchanged a smile, broken by Bev's voice bellowing from the front of the house. "Emma!"

"I better go see what she wants. Come on, I'll introduce you."

"Not today. I'm late as it is." He hesitated for a moment, as if he were going to say something else. Then he shook his head. "I'll see you at eight."

"Right." I hurried off, expecting him to head in the same direction I did. When I looked back from the corner of the house, he was already gone.

Chapter Three

I left my part-time job at the art supply store when it closed at eight and hurried down the block and around the corner to Carolina Coffee. I was nearly at the door when Adam appeared at my elbow. "I wasn't sure you'd show up," he said.

"Of course I would. We had a—," I almost said date, and then realized how pushy I sounded. Adam seemed old-fashioned, so I changed my words to "an agreement."

He held the door open for me, and we walked in. I had a second's thought that he should teach manners to the other guys in town. I was as likely to have the door slam in my face as to have it held open, but mostly it was my ex's friends who hit me with doors. If I reacted in any way, they called me "Psycho-babe."

I ordered a decaf with a turkey sandwich and paid for my own. Adam followed me to the table without ordering anything. Apparently, my guess about him being homeless wasn't too far off the mark. "Don't you want anything?"

"No. I'm fine."

"Here. Let me get you a coffee. My treat."

His face said he wanted to refuse, but then he smiled and said, "Thank you."

I got him a small regular and brought it over. We sat down at a booth with our coffees and an uneasy silence fell between us. Then the bell over the shop door chimed and in walked two scruffy men. My groan was audible.

"You know them?" Adam asked.

"Good friends of my ex. Especially Gary." I kept my gaze on Adam.

"Ex?"

"Ex-husband. He's a construction worker when he's not being a layabout, and so are they."

"Em, who's your new squeeze?" Gary Lofton said as he sauntered up to our table.

The result would have been worse if I ignored them. "Adam, this is Gary and Sam. Guys, this is Adam."

"How long you been dating Psycho-babe?" Gary asked.

Adam gave him a steely gaze. "Emma is a friend. I don't like people speaking badly of my friends."

"You've got pretty poor taste in friends," Gary said.

Sam looked from one man to the other, didn't like what he was seeing any more than I did, and put a hand on Gary's arm. "Let's get our coffee, man."

"Sounds like a good idea," Adam agreed.

"I'm just trying to protect you from Psycho-babe."

"That's getting old, Gary. Go away," I said. Gary was probably my cheating ex's best buddy. Everyone probably would have let things drop if not for Gary. And of course,

Tim, my ex.

He stood over me, smiling as if he was planning something I wouldn't like.

"Gary. Go. Away."

Sam said, "Come on, Gary," and walked off.

Silence had stretched a little thin before Adam said, "You've got yourself an admirer, Emma. Gary here can't keep his eyes off you."

I glanced up to see Gary staring with hatred at Adam who was smirking at him.

"Psycho-babe? I don't think so."

"Reminds me of all the crushes we used to have in grade school. Next, he'll be saying it's you who can't get enough of him," Adam continued as if Gary hadn't spoken.

"He's already done that," I said, remembering an incident when Gary and Tim had been by the house to move out more of his gear. And left with some things that were mine.

"I rest my case. He's got a crush on you, Emma." Adam was grinning broadly now.

Gary looked ready to hit him. Adam had tensed, appearing ready to respond if he struck. "What's your name?" Gary snarled.

"Adam Chadwick. And yours?"

"Gary Lofton."

"I'll remember," Adam said in a tone men use to warn each other off.

"You'd better," Gary replied.

Sam returned, grabbed Gary, and led him over to the counter to order their coffees to go.

I looked at Adam, shook my head, and said, "Sorry."

"You don't need to apologize. He does."

"He won't. Don't worry about it."

"Does he act like that every time he sees you?"

"It's worse if he's with my ex."

Adam put a hand out and touched mine with a whisper-soft glance. "What happened?"

"Tim, my ex-husband, cheated on me repeatedly. I confronted him and the current woman in a bar one night. In front of his friends. They nicknamed me Psycho-babe and told every guy in town about it. It became a big game. Embarrass Emma. How come they didn't tell you?"

In a very serious tone, he said, "I don't hang out with pond scum."

Fortunately, I didn't have coffee in my mouth, or it would have sprayed over Adam as I laughed.

The ice broken, we talked like old friends. I barely noticed when Sam and Gary left, although I couldn't miss Gary watching Adam with a narrow-eyed, thoughtful glance. Adam had only told me a few stories old man Duffy had told him about Summerduck when the staff ushered us out at closing time.

I thought it odd Adam's coffee was untouched.

Then we stood awkwardly on the sidewalk. "I'll walk you home," Adam said.

"I'm this way." I turned to walk toward the Fishhook River, past the stores and restaurants that made up our downtown. A few people were out enjoying the night air, but now that darkness had fallen, most were inside their expensive apartments above the stores, on their equally expensive boats, or had gone to wherever home was.

Most of the bugs were flying around the streetlights, but I still had to swat at a few mosquitoes. Adam appeared to be one of those fortunate people that don't attract insects.

We reached the river by way of the park and walked along the brick walkway by the sea wall.

Adam stopped and leaned on the railing. "Every time I walk along here, I'm struck again with how beautiful this is." We looked at the crescent moon high in the sky.

"It is. It's even better when there's a full moon and just a few clouds. Then you get the moonlight shining on the water alternating with the moon glowing in the sky through the clouds."

"It'll be a new moon day after tomorrow," Adam said, adding in a regretful voice, "but this isn't getting you home."

"Bev wants me back at the house early tomorrow while she deals with another painter and a carpenter."

"That house is going to take a lot of work. I didn't realize until the yard was cleared just how sad it looked."

He said it with such feeling that I couldn't help but study his face. "The old Chadwick place means a lot to you, doesn't it?"

"It's a prime example of the architecture of its day. It used to sit proudly at the end of the street."

"End? It's in the middle of the block."

"Those smaller houses on the same side were built later, when Walnut Street was extended." He gave me a grin. "Look it up in the library. You said you like to hang out at the library."

I laughed. "I did say that." We reached the end of the public walkway along the river where the path became a sidewalk bent by ancient tree roots in front of a house. I looked through their side yard to the river. "What a marvelous view they have out the back."

"All the houses on this side of the street have gorgeous views." He waved one arm expansively. "Of course, whenever we get a hurricane, they become part of the view."

"Have you been through a hurricane here?" I asked, suddenly aware I still knew precious little about him, despite our conversation.

"A few. You?"

"Yes." I pointed. "I'm down the next street. I rent the upstairs. The fire chief and his wife live downstairs. His wife is my aunt and when I found myself homeless after—after the divorce, she had me move in over them in the apartment their daughter lived in before she moved to Raleigh." No reason to mention a short stay in a mental facility before I moved in.

"Do you like living in the upstairs of an old house?"

I gave him an *are you nuts* look. "I love old houses. I love the whole downtown area. I grew up in a turn-of-the-century house on Oak Street. It was crowded and the floors sloped, but I loved it."

"Lots to love about old houses." His mouth quirked. "Old wiring. Old plumbing. Leaky roofs. Lots of repairs."

"Which makes my rent cheap." We turned down my street at right angles to the river and stopped in front of the third house. The front yard was little more than a row of neatly trimmed bushes and Aunt Jean's flower beds. I felt like I could reach out the windows in my apartment and touch the houses on either side.

"The Wilson place," Adam said approvingly.

"I thought next door was the Wilson house."

"It is, also. When their son got married, the parents built this house next door to them on the land where they'd kept their cows and hens. By then people were no longer keeping livestock inside the town limit so the land was available. Rumor had it that Mrs. Wilson senior didn't trust her new daughter-in-law and wanted to keep an eye on her."

"How do you know all this?"

"The library. Talking to the old people in town like Mr. Duffy. I'm naturally curious and I like history."

By now we were standing on the steps up to the wide front porch. Chief Bobby, my landlord, must have heard us, because the floodlights came on. Adam put up a hand to shield his eyes and said, "Looks like it's time to leave. Thanks for a lovely evening."

I smiled. "I've enjoyed this evening. Have a good night."

"I'll see you around." He grinned at me, that contented smile that he had, and walked into the night. With the flood lights on, he disappeared as soon as he stepped beyond the glaring light shining in my face.

* * *

The next morning, I took Bev's place at the old house while she went to a board meeting of her family business. I played the part of her general contractor while I showed the workmen what they were bidding on.

I was glad her family's transport business had turned into a gold mine. That way she was able to afford the Chadwick house and hire me. The business had also paid to send her older brother to an Ivy League school, where he'd roomed with Roger. Bev was happy about how that turned out, too.

The first cloud on the horizon appeared with Bubba Ward as he loped around the outside of the house, his torn T-shirt showing off bronzed skin pulled tight over lean muscles. He banged on clapboards and poked at foundation stones, all the while murmuring to himself.

I went inside to show the plumber what was planned on a complete kitchen overhaul and dividing one bathroom upstairs into two. When I came back out, Ward ambled up to me, rubbing his hand over his stubbled cheeks.

"You know about the termites?"

"Yes. The plan is to have the damage repaired after the place is fumigated. We didn't expect you to be available for the next month, so we thought we'd ask for a quote now and get on your waiting list."

He scratched behind his ear. "And you said they want insulation added to the walls."

"Yes." Why did I have a feeling this was leading to something neither Bev nor I wanted to hear?

"The foundation isn't going to hold any extra weight."

Here it came. "What do you mean?"

He scratched his elbow. "Foundation's crumbling. The cement between the rocks is turning to powder. Some of the rocks aren't big enough. There's just not enough there to hold this place up, not after all this time. It's gonna slip, or sink, or collapse."

Bev wasn't going to want to hear this, but Roger would just tell her to do whatever made her happy with the house. I feared that might include killing the messenger.

"What do you recommend, Mr. Ward?"

"Get in a structural engineer. He'll want to jack the house up and rebuild the foundation. Then after the place is fumigated, I'll be able to replace all the rotted wood." He patted the faded old boards on the side of the house. "It's a good, sturdy house all told. It can be a showplace. But it's gonna take some time and a pile of money."

Bev wasn't going to like that message.

I didn't get the shriek of dismay I expected. Her voice was much colder and angrier over the phone as she said, "Don't agree to anything. I'll get a structural engineer."

Once I'd taken care of calling Bev and seen off the plumber and Bubba, I went to the library and walked into the local history room. Dave was on duty as always, eating a sandwich behind his desk. "1904," I said, smiling brightly.

"That's more specific than people usually get. What are you looking for?" Dave sounded impressed.

"A murder that took place at the house my friend Bev

Myers just bought."

The sandwich went down with a thud. "Which house?" he asked as his fingers ran along the keyboard of his computer.

"The old Chadwick place on Walnut."

"Okay, it's in the index. Everything was moved over to microfiche years ago. Come on." Leaving his sandwich uncovered and unguarded, Dave leaned heavily on his cane as he led me into the microfiche section. After a short search, he had three files in his hand. "Start with these."

He turned back to resume his lunch. I sat down at one of the two machines and began to read. The first file was the local newspaper for the year 1904. I skimmed through, glancing at ads for farm implements, church services, and corsets, before I hit pay dirt.

The lead story for the June 17th issue was "Fight causes death of local lawyer." I skimmed through the story the first time, learning the fight had occurred on the previous afternoon in the barn. The deceased, Adam Chadwick, had died from a stab wound to the abdomen. He had also had a head injury. His twin brother, Benjamin, had been stabbed in the arm with a pitchfork.

Chapter Four

The article went on to say Benjamin Chadwick ran the family farm and lumber mill business while Adam practiced law. A disagreement over a family matter led to an altercation. Their sister, Clarissa, heard the argument and went outside to find Adam dead and Benjamin injured. Benjamin said Adam had struck first and he had only been defending himself.

Various quotes from neighbors and judges spoke of Adam's sharp mind and sense of humor, his popularity around the courthouse and his kindness to all. He was called honest, hardworking, well-mannered and trustworthy. There were no quotes from Benjamin or Clarissa. Was it because they were grieving or because they couldn't say anything nice about their brother?

I looked through the issue, but I found no mention of charges being filed or funeral arrangements.

Staring at the windows across the room, I wondered at the name. Adam Chadwick. The same as my friend. Perhaps a name that kept being passed down through the family. Or maybe Adam was just a popular boy's name.

The next issue, June 24th, contained a small box on the front page, apparently added at the last moment, saying Benjamin Chadwick had died of lockjaw just before press time. The story on Adam's funeral took up page three. The service had been on Saturday in St. George Episcopal Church with the burial in the town cemetery in the Chadwick family plot. The story went on in overblown detail to say everyone in town was there and how much Adam Chadwick would be missed. The only people not in attendance were Benjamin Chadwick, who was home suffering from injuries sustained in the fight, and Miss Sarah May Elliott, who'd been the children's nursemaid and was now caring for Benjamin in his illness.

That explained why no charges had been filed.

The next issue, July 1st, was full of plans for the big Fourth of July celebration with a parade down Broad Street to the courthouse and a picnic on the grounds of both St. George Episcopal Church and First Baptist Church.

I tried to picture how Summerduck looked at that time. The Baptists had added on a huge Sunday school building to the back of their sanctuary, and the Episcopalians had put in a gymnasium. The churches were back to back facing parallel streets, so they must have had a huge empty area between them one hundred and some years before, big enough for the whole town to come to the picnic.

Dragging my attention back to the over-bright

microfiche, I found an account of Benjamin's funeral on page five. It was written in an equally flowery style, but there weren't many quotes from mourners. I noticed the quotes said nothing but said it tactfully. It didn't appear the paper was as interested in Benjamin's funeral or the town as upset by his passing.

I flipped back to look at dates. The two men were twins, born thirty-one years before. It seemed like an awful waste of two lives.

The second microfiche file contained legal documents from that time. Interestingly, neither man left the house, their share of the family business or anything else to their brother. Both made their sister their primary beneficiary. The wills were five years old in Adam's case and seven in Benjamin's. It didn't take a genius to guess their relationship had been rocky from long before the day of their lethal fight.

The last microfiche held a pamphlet, written in the forties, about the houses in the historic district. I knew this was the time when interest was beginning to grow in the history of our town. I skimmed through it until I came to the Chadwick house. "Built in the 1880s by wealthy mill owner and farmer Nathaniel Chadwick, this impressive two-story and attic residence originally sat at the end of Walnut Street. Nathaniel died in 1898, leaving the house to his older son, Adam. When Adam died in 1904 under tragic circumstances, he left the house to his sister, Clarissa. In 1905, the adjoining land, owned by the Chadwicks, was sold for three building lots and Walnut Street was extended." No mention was made of Benjamin or the "tragic circumstances."

I returned the microfiche to Dave, who was now working on an apple and reading. "Is there any record of a police report or autopsy?"

"Not here, but you could try the police department. We 'fiched a lot of old records for them and gave everything back about ten years ago. I don't know if there was anything that old in the stuff they gave us."

"Really?" I'd never read about an old criminal case except in the local paper. These deaths obviously hadn't reached the point of a trial, but there must have been a police report. "One more thing. Has anyone else asked to look at these same sources?"

Dave gave a snort. "Not in years. People act like nothing happened in Summerduck after the Civil War until the Civil Rights movement."

"How about years ago?"

"I've only been on this desk for the past six years. Before then, who knows?"

I gave him a smile. "Thanks for the help, Dave."

The new police station, a modern red-brick building, sat a quick three-block walk from the library on the other side of the railroad tracks. Even in the summer heat I was there in five minutes, presenting my slightly sweaty self at the front desk.

I was soon handed over to an administrative assistant. The blue in the print of her dress picked up the blue in her eyes, and the gray in the background of the silky material matched the gray in her hair. Since I wore a

T-shirt and shorts for spending time in an unairconditioned house on a hot day, I felt reminded of the sartorial shortcomings my ex used to point out.

We moved to her office, where I made my request.

"Why would you like to see these records?"

"There's a disagreement between a homeowner and the Historical Society about an old structure and whether it can be taken down. The reason the Historical Society is giving is an event that took place in that shed, barn, whatever it is, in 1904. It was a police matter, and the homeowner wants to know if the event was of sufficient historical interest to require her to restore the shed, rather than tear it down."

The woman smiled. "You have me interested. What was the incident?"

"Accident, double murder, no one is quite sure over a hundred years later. But it was a sudden death, and violent, so I would think a police report would have been written."

She nodded and handed me a form. "Write your request on this, and I'll see what I can do. I know we have microfiche of old records, but I'm not certain how far they go back."

I filled out the form, rose, and shook her hand. "Thank you."

As I left the building, I heard my name called. Looking toward the parking lot, I saw Sergeant Mike Randall striding toward me. There was no doubt I was his target. My immediate reaction was to run. Randall meant trouble.

At least, he meant trouble for me. If he wasn't leering at my shorts, he'd tease me about something. Anything to get on my nerves.

I took a deep breath and remained where I was. When he reached me, he said, "Hey, there, Sugarbear. Want to get some lunch?"

That surprised me. "I've already eaten," I lied.

"Then come along while I eat."

"No, thank you."

He smirked. "Then I don't suppose you want to hear what I learned about your friend Chadwick and the house the Myers bought."

That had my attention. I squared off with him, livid. "You've been investigating my friends?"

Randall put his hands up, playfully acting frightened. He was bigger and stronger than me. And he was armed. "Whoa, now, Em. It wasn't me. Come have lunch with me, and I'll tell you all about it."

I nodded. And the first time he tried anything, I'd bend back his fingers. If I got a chance.

We walked to a popular sub shop on the edge of downtown while he complimented my beaded hair combs. Not something I heard every day, but I knew Mike's Uncle Bobby and Aunt Jean were big on manners.

I studied him as we talked of the weather. It was predictably hot and humid, but any Southerner can make a conversation last five minutes built of nothing more than the predictable. Bev had said Randall was good-looking, and she was probably right. He wore his hair too short to tell if it was still the pretty auburn shade it had been in school. He had a nice build and obviously kept himself in shape by beating up on suspects or running them down or whatever he did for exercise.

At least he had the good manners to hold the door for me as we entered the shop, although I suspected it was to get a good look at my backside. We sat down in the rear of the eatery, Randall as always with his back to the wall. I ordered a salad. He ordered a roast beef sub, but wonder of wonders, he changed the usual fries that came with it for a fruit salad.

"I didn't realize you were health conscious," I said, giving him high marks for something positive.

"Got to keep my girlish figure," he said, wiping out the good impression he'd made.

I lowered my voice. "Who's investigating my friends?"

"A citizen asked what we had on an Adam Chadwick."

"Gary Lofton."

He grinned. "You didn't hear that from me. The description matched a man people in the historic district have seen around the old Chadwick place."

"And?"

"That's it."

"What do you mean, that's it?"

"Sugarbear, the guy doesn't exist. He's under the radar. No driver's license, no record, no job, no address. Curious, someone went a little farther. No military record, no birth certificate under that name, no fishing license, and no one at the bank branches in town have heard of him. In fact, no one in town has heard of him."

"I have. Gary has. I'm sure others have, too." As I'd suspected, he was homeless.

"You've met someone, but his name isn't Adam Chadwick."

Our lunches arrived and we dug in. As soon as he finished eating, Mike signaled for the check. He pulled out a ten and handed it to the waitress. "Keep the change, doll."

I wondered if the tip was sufficient payment for the leer he gave her or the obvious peek down her blouse.

He turned back to me and said, "I have to go back on duty. I just wanted to warn you. Stay away from him until we find out who he really is and why he's using an assumed name."

"And the Myers' house?"

"That's about the only place in town your mystery man has been seen. Beware of him, Sugarbear."

I turned and watched him stride out of the shop, others stepping out of his way. Then I looked at the remains of my salad. I'd lost my appetite. Adam had more of a connection to Bev's house than he'd told me.

Why had he lied to me about his name?

* * *

A few days later, Bev called and begged me to come over to the Chadwick house with tears in her voice. I dropped the costume I was sewing for the play and hurried over.

Strange metal contraptions had been set around the

foundation, and Bev stood in the front yard, staring at the house and looking ready to commit murder. "Bubba Ward was right. The foundation's crumbling, so we're having to jack the house up and put cement and stone around the foundation inside and out to take care of the problem. And then it has to be fumigated. Only after that can we can start working on the house itself."

"Roger must be unhappy," was the first thing I thought and it slipped out.

She glared at me. "So am I, but he's furious. If he could find a way to get out of the deal he would, but the lawyer says the house, and the loan, are ours."

"He checked?" Never a good sign.

"Yes. He's never loved the house as much as I do." Bev looked grief-stricken. "He's just not in love with Summerduck yet."

I put a hand on her arm. "Don't let this house come between you two. Roger's a good guy. How long will this part take?"

"Anywhere from a week to a month, and we can't go inside until the work is completed."

"I'm sorry, Bev, but in the grand scheme of things, a month isn't very long. You'll laugh about this someday."

Her fury found a new target. Me. "No, I won't laugh about this, and yes, a month is a long time, so don't talk nonsense."

I gave her a wincing smile. "It always sounded great when my grandmother said it."

"That's because your grandmother was a nice old lady and she was talking about things like boys and dances and school projects." When I opened my mouth, Bev held up her hand. "No. Not another word."

We stood together, watching the workmen build the supports for repairing the foundation. "It reminds me of when I wore braces. My mouth looked like that. Bev, I am sorry. But see, the braces made me beautiful." I gave her a big smile.

I was relieved to see her smile as she swung her purse around to hit me in the shoulder.

* * *

I received a call from the Police Department Public Affairs office a few days later. Their records were incomplete before World War II. They had nothing for 1904. And there was no mention of Chadwicks in any year in their old files which only went back to the end of World War I.

Chapter Five

Two weeks after I took the call from the police, and despite questioning Dave on several occasions, I still couldn't find anything more about the Chadwick family and house. I focused all my energy on my painting and learning my lines for our new play, *Long Day's Journey into Night*, to be presented in early October and gave up any hope of discovering more about the killings in 1904.

During that time, I'd looked for Adam along the river walk, in front of my house, by the coffee shop, or wherever I happened to be, but I never saw him. I wondered if he would reappear or if he'd left Summerduck for good. I was starting to forget about him and his gentle eyes.

One place I did not go during the entire time the foundation work was underway was to Bev's new house. Seeing the stately old building surrounded by metal framework was painful. The house wasn't mine, but I felt like I had a stake in the success of its restoration.

Bev told me she couldn't look at it either. It was too awful.

* * *

Whatever magic the builders performed on the foundation of the old Chadwick place during the hot dry spell worked. The jacks came down; the city inspector was happy. Bev was overjoyed that one roadblock had been cleared.

Finally, on a hot day at the end of summer, I stood in the rear of the Chadwick house with Bev and Walter Clapp, the exterminator. All the bracing was removed from the foundation. Every door, window, and crack had been sealed with tape the day before and now noxious gases were ready to be pumped into the house to kill the bugs living inside.

Stripped of the overgrowth and sitting on a new, sturdy foundation made of cinderblocks clad with rock, the untended old house above the footings looked sadder than ever.

Next to us in a yard of dirt and trampled weeds, the pump was ready to force poisonous gas from the tanks. The equipment was fed electricity by a thick, orange extension cord that ran through the curtain of heavy plastic that draped the house. Before the tent was in place, I'd seen the cord running through the back doorway to the electrical panel in the back hall. A flexible hose entered the same way, dispensing lethal gas.

I wondered if it would remove the face in the upstairs window.

"How long until all that gas is cleared out and we can have people working inside?" Bev asked.

"We'll open the house on Saturday morning, but don't

schedule anyone until Monday. The smell will linger." Mr. Clapp answered while bent over, reading one of the gauges.

I swatted a no-see-um, knowing I'd have a small round red mark on my skin shortly from its bite. Too bad Clapp couldn't gas the outside, too.

"I'll come by Saturday morning and help you open up the windows once you've got the tent off," Bev said, "and so will Emma."

Okay. Glad to know my Saturday was planned. I swatted another gnat. "Then I think you should have Bubba begin demolition of the rotten boards on the outside on Monday. Get rid of the bugs, inside and out, as fast as possible. Then the improvements can begin." And I couldn't wait to begin painting walls and stripping varnish and stain, and ordering around plumbers and electricians.

Standing there staring at the house made me fall in love with it and its possibilities once more.

Bev and Clapp remained in the backyard talking while he inspected his tanks. I walked off to return home. I'd just reached the front of the house when Adam came up beside me.

I jumped a foot, since he'd been nowhere around a moment before, and because of what Sergeant Mike Randall had told me.

"I didn't mean to scare you, Emma. I'm sorry."

"No problem. I just didn't see or hear you. You move very quietly." My heart kept hammering on my chest, but looking into his baby blue eyes, I suspected my pulse rate was raised by more than shock.

"So I've been told."

I could believe that. "By whom?"

"My siblings. Why all the questions?"

I looked for a different answer than *who are you really*? "I haven't seen you around lately."

"I haven't seen you, either. Guess we've both been busy."

There was no answer for that, but the doubts Mike had planted made me wonder where Adam had been busy, and what he had been doing.

"Okay, Emma, what's wrong?"

"What's wrong?" My voice sounded a little screechy.

He gave me a dry look. "You're acting really nervous."

"I was wondering what your profession is. Your job. What you do for a living."

"Afraid I'm an axe murderer? No such luck." He grinned at me in such an odd way a shiver ran along my neck despite the heat. "I do odd jobs. Set my own schedule."

"Do what makes you happy," I suggested.

His gaze turned to the house with sadness written in his eyes. "I wish." I felt like I could reach out and touch his despair.

After a moment he turned to me and shook off his melancholy. "Sometimes we must be ruthless in our pursuit of happiness. And I've never particularly liked being ruthless."

Uneasy in his company for the first time, I said, "I

have to go, but I'll be back here Saturday opening windows and whatever else Bev wants me to do."

"Great. I hope I see you then. Good day, Emma."

I climbed up onto the porch and he walked down the street. When I looked back ten seconds later, he was gone. Adam Chadwick, or whoever he was, moved fast.

It made me wonder what he was running from. And for some reason, I wondered if he was a burglar.

* * *

Saturday morning, I came dressed in old shorts, a T-shirt with paint on it, and work boots. There was no way I was ruining decent clothes in a dusty house with no air conditioning in our sultry late-August weather. I'd clipped my hair on top of my head in an effort to save me from sweaty strands clinging to my neck. Bev arrived carrying sweet tea and biscuits, so I forgave her taking over my Saturday on a day when the weather made my clothes stick to my skin even before we began work.

We walked around to the back of the house together, munching on breakfast. Bev remembered I preferred ham and cheese biscuits, no doubt trying to bribe me for the work ahead. The pumps had been shut off, the electric cord rolled up, the hose removed, the tent removed, and the back door opened, but there was no sign of Clapp. We walked into the kitchen and while Bev set our sweet teas in the grumbling old refrigerator, I stripped off the sealing material and opened the kitchen and pantry windows.

"The house stinks." I should have thought to bring a scarf to wrap around my nose and mouth.

"I guess he hasn't had the machine turned off long. Let's get some windows open. I'm going to choke on these gases." Bev headed for the dining room.

I walked toward the front door but never reached it. Walter Clapp lay in the front hallway, tied up and gagged by sealing material. He shifted his head along the floor to stare at me with huge, unblinking eyes that shouted his fear.

I bent down and began to unwrap the flexible gray fabric, untying neatly tied knots. "What happened? Who did this to you?"

"I don't know. I must have tripped on the sealing tape, fallen and hit my head."

"This neatly? Someone did this to you. What happened?"

"I don't know." His hands were free and he was helping me pull away the tape. "I have to get out of here."

"Did you hit your head? Let me see." I tried to examine his head, but he immediately jerked his head away. Just from the quick glance, I didn't see any blood or bumps.

"Leave me alone. I need to get out of this house."

"What about opening the house?"

"You do it. I'm out of here." He shoved the rest of the sealing material away, clambered up and hurried toward the kitchen.

"We can call the police from outside." I chased after him.

"We don't need police. There's nothing to report. I

just want to leave."

I burst into the kitchen on Clapp's heels to find Bev leaning against the sink, drinking her iced tea. "I'll send you my bill," Mr. Clapp said and kept going out the back hall.

Bev joined me as we caught up to him. He snatched up his equipment in the backyard, slinging the electric cord and flexible hose over his shoulder.

"How did that happen?" I demanded.

"How did *what* happen?" Bev asked.

"Nothing." Clapp carried the load around to his truck.

"I found him in the front hall bound and gagged by sealing foam strips and tape."

"Was it an accident?" Bev sounded hopeful.

"No. It had to have been done by a person." I pictured the way I'd found him. "A person standing behind him to bind and gag him. And the knots were neatly tied."

"Could he have done it himself?" Bev asked, a trace of hope still lingering in her voice.

"No. Someone else was in there. And Mr. Clapp looked terrified." I'd never forget how panicked he looked. "I wonder what kind of trouble he's in."

Clapp was back in a moment for the other load, including his wheeled gas tank and engine.

"Who attacked you, Mr. Clapp?" Bev asked.

"No one. Don't you understand? No one did that. I'll send my bill. Good luck with your house," he grumbled as he walked away.

"What is he talking about?" Bev asked.

I shrugged. And then I thought of Adam Chadwick.

Was he dangerous? We walked around to the front yard and watched Mr. Clapp peel out from the curb in his panel van.

There was still no sign of Adam. When I glanced up at the window, the man's face was there, smiling.

* * *

We walked around to the back and returned to work, both of us silent with our thoughts. We circled the downstairs, stripping off sealant and opening those few windows Mr. Clapp hadn't reached before he was attacked. I finished the front door while Bev busied herself in the study.

We checked the upstairs room by room together. They had already been opened. When we reached the big bedroom in the front, I hesitated before walking in. Bev charged ahead, and when I looked, these windows hadn't been touched. Bev had already untaped most of one window.

I tiptoed in, afraid to stir up the malevolent force that had thrown me out of the room once and leered at me from the window. This time there was nothing. No chest pains. No vanishing figure. I helped Bev open the windows without incident, but I rushed to leave the room. Just in case.

Once we were done, we returned to the first floor. Bev dusted her hands off and said, "There. We've got every window opened. The smell will be gone by Monday, and the electricians and the painters can get started."

I was surprised. "You're starting to paint inside

already? I thought that'd be the last thing you did."

"Not inside, outside. Mr. Ward has us on his schedule to replace all the rotten boards starting Monday. As the new boards go up, they'll need primer and then everything will need two coats of paint to keep the house from falling down."

"What color did you decide on? I know Roger wanted white." Nice, operating-room-sterile white.

"The grayish-blue you suggested. The painter said once they seal the new boards, it will make painting easier if they aren't putting white over white."

"So, you don't need me for a while." That was okay with me. I had rehearsals coming up for the play and I wanted to put some new items in the gift shop where I sold on commission.

I was also disappointed that I hadn't seen Adam again. Mike Randall was right. The only place I'd met Adam, except for our one date, was here outside the Chadwick house.

Finally, a guy who seemed to listen to me, to like me, to enjoy my company, and he was a drifter who'd be gone from my life before I ever learned anything about him. Maybe he found out Gary Lofton had the police do a records search on him. Maybe he was an Army deserter so there were no VA records on him. Maybe he was a fugitive because, as he said, he'd been ruthless in his search for happiness. Maybe—who knew?

I remembered Walter Clapp lying trussed up and terrified on the floor, sealing material wrapped around his body and mouth while his eyes looked around in panic. Maybe Adam had attacked him. Maybe Adam was an assumed name, and Mr. Clapp recognized him.

"I'm sure I'll be calling you soon. And Emma, I appreciate all your help," Bev said, unaware I'd been thinking of someone besides her.

We locked up the front and went out the back, the smell now weakening. It was as if Walter Clapp had never been inside the house.

I'd only walked a block away from the old Chadwick place after parting company from Bev when Adam silently appeared at my side. I jumped as he jogged up next to me. "You have to stop sneaking up on me like that," I snapped.

"I'm sorry. When I came over this morning, I didn't see you but I saw that workman rush away. I was afraid something had happened to you." Adam slowed his steps to match mine on the uneven concrete sidewalk.

"Not me. The exterminator. Mr. Clapp. He was left tied up in the front hall."

Adam stopped next to an old maple with roots that had broken up fifteen feet of sidewalk. Banging his fist on the bark, he said, "Sweet piddle. Excuse me, Emma."

"I thought the same thing." Well, actually I thought in four-letter words, but the sentiment was the same. Then I stared into his eyes. "What do you know about what is happening in that house?"

"Nothing. It's been an unlucky house."

"What do you mean, unlucky?"

He lowered his gaze as he shook his head.

The silence continued between us before I said, "Where have you been the last couple of weeks?"

"Here and there. Around town."

I kept watching his lovely blue eyes shift their gaze from one spot to another. "Doing odd jobs? What kind of odd jobs?"

He looked at his worn work boots so I could no longer read his expression. "Nothing important. Nothing exciting like your life, starring in plays and painting and such."

"I don't do anything important or interesting."

"If you truly believed that, you'd leave here and go somewhere else. I know you, Emma. You want what you do to matter." He looked up and held my gaze.

I blinked first. His certainty bothered me. "Why do you think you know me?"

"Because we're alike. At least, I used to be like you. What I did needed to be helpful. Useful."

Finally, I might learn something about him. "What did you do that was useful?"

"I was involved in civic affairs, advocating for the underdog, trying to help the poor and oppressed." He glanced at me and said, "Don't think I was a saint. I had enough money to allow me to be generous with my time."

I blinked again. This time in surprise. "Still, that was noble of you."

He snorted. "Noble. No. I think it was my way of being a rabble-rouser. Can't picture me as a rabble-rouser, can you?"

I couldn't. He was so kind, so calm. "What made you

change?"

"Death."

Chapter Six

Adam's answer left me gaping at him with my mouth open. "What happened?" I blurted out when I found my voice.

He turned away from me, his head down. "I don't want to talk about it. It's still too painful."

Could that be why he was living off the grid? Because of sorrow? Or guilt, a little voice said in my ear.

He started to walk again in the direction of my upstairs apartment. I joined him, neither of us speaking. When we reached the corner, he spoke very quietly, so quietly I wasn't certain if he were talking to himself or to me. "I wasn't at fault."

I decided to take the opening. All right, I wanted to know more about him. Was Adam who he appeared to be, an intelligent but damaged man, or was he a killer, stalking our town for reasons I couldn't fathom? "Then why are you living away from everyone? If you're not at fault, no one is blaming you."

He smiled, shaking his head. "Oh, Emma, I wish it were that simple."

"It is. You must live somewhere. That would provide

an address so you could get a steady job. Apply for benefits. You could start living on the grid again."

I watched him as I made suggestions for beginning his life over, and he just smiled and shook his head.

"Are you happy living the way you are?" I asked.

His expression turned angry in an instant. He clenched his fists and walked a few steps away from me. Then he returned and said, "No. And it's none of your business. I knew this was a mistake, but I couldn't help myself."

"What's a mistake?"

He opened his fists and stared at me for a moment. "Thinking I could have a nice, simple friendship with a pretty young lady. That's what got me into this mess in the first place."

"What mess?"

"Emma." His tone of voice told me I'd overstepped the bounds of friendship.

I stared back, feeling guilty. Instead of being a friend, I was interfering in his life. "I'm sorry. What you do and where you live is none of my business. I'd like to be your friend."

He tilted his head and stared into my eyes. "No more trying to solve my problems?"

It was my turn to smile and shake my head. "No more." I hated when my family and friends tried to do that, even though I understood why they'd put me in the psychiatric ward. I was curious, but Adam had a right to his privacy.

"In that case, I plan to watch the Fishhook River tonight when it gets to be dusk." He gave me a hopeful look. "Shall I meet you about eight thirty along the river path?"

I felt my smile widen. The town of Summerduck was situated at the confluence of two rivers, the Fishhook and the Wales. The river walk ran from along the Wales River by the marina around the point and up the Fishhook past the downtown business area. "Yes. Meet you just upstream from the Porthole Restaurant?"

He grinned back. "I'll see you there." He started to walk away and I headed to my apartment.

I turned around to ask him if he'd like to get some coffee first, but he'd already disappeared up the side street.

* * *

Adam was already on the river path heading toward me when I crossed the street in front of the restaurant. I waved and he hurried in my direction. The street lights along the path were already lit, leaving circles of light on the concrete and brick walk and reflecting off the shiny metal railings. I leaned on the railing and waited for him to reach me, letting the river breeze ruffle my beaded top.

Okay, so I put on my nicest shorts and sandals and a bright top that went well with my skin tone. I have the right to dream, don't I?

"Beautiful, isn't it?" he asked, looking at the last streaks of pink fading in the night and the stars shining above the house lights across the river. A powerboat passed us going downstream, its running lights shimmering off the waves.

"It is. And so peaceful."

"Or would be if the boat would cut off his motor."

"You like sailboats better?" I asked.

I could see his smile in the street lamp. "They're elegant, graceful, and quiet. But even they now have motors. Can't stand in the way of progress, I guess."

"What do you mean, 'even they now have motors'? They've had them for years."

"I was thinking of the Vikings, the Phoenicians, the Venetians. They sailed, or they rowed. Quietly," he replied.

I grinned at him. "Bet their rowers would be jealous of our ship engines."

He laughed. "Bet you're right."

His laugh told me he'd forgiven me for trying to redirect his life. I should have learned by now that guys don't like that. My ex hated for me to make suggestions about anything that touched on whether or not he did something he wanted to do. Usually that something was going out with the guys, which then led to picking up chicks. As a married man, he went back to his old ways within weeks.

Somehow, I couldn't imagine Adam behaving like that.

And that led me to imagining Bev warning me not to fall for another man on the basis of his pretty eyes.

"Penny for your thoughts," broke into my reverie.

"I was thinking you have pretty eyes."

He turned away from the water and stared at me for a long pause. "No one ever said that to me before."

"Good."

"Good?" he asked.

"I'm glad I'm the first."

His smile turned sad. "It's been a long time since anyone was my first."

The river was dark now that night had fallen. No boats passed us and the new moon and the stars didn't reflect on the water. The single light that showed me Adam's face was from a nearby streetlamp. His expression could only be described as longing. I suspected he longed for something he knew he couldn't have.

I hoped that thing he couldn't have wasn't me or my friendship.

The breeze off the river chilled my skin and blew my hair into my face. At least it kept the insects away. He reached over and used one finger to brush it back so gently I didn't feel him touch me.

"Come on." He began walking up-stream along the path and I walked beside him, feeling the cool air on my face and arms. It was darker along here. I almost hoped he'd kiss me.

He finally stopped along the railing where trees blocked most of the light from the streetlamps and turned to face me. "Emma, you are a wonderful person. I don't want you to get your hopes up. I won't change."

I tried to interrupt him, but he put an index finger over my lips. At least I imagined he had. He moved it away so fast I didn't feel his skin brush my lips.

"I won't change. I can't change. It's complicated. Just know I'm trying to protect you and your friend."

"From what?"

He studied my face. I didn't know how he could see much in the dim light, but he seemed to come to a decision. "You don't know."

"Don't know what?"

"The Chadwick house is haunted. By a malevolent spirit."

Okay. Adam was crazy. Hopefully, he was a harmless crazy. "I've heard stories about ghosts living in half the houses downtown. Great stories, but that's all they are. Stories."

"Who do you think attacked the exterminator?"

"Mr. Clapp? Someone who followed him in, perhaps to rob him, perhaps someone who held a grudge against him. The Chadwick house is in a nice area, but it isn't far from a slum with drug deals and all sorts of misery and violence. That seems like the best possibility."

He gave me a wry smile. "What about the face you see in the bedroom window?"

"There's no one in there. The house has been checked multiple times. It's a trick of the light on old glass. It has to be."

"Believe that if you want, but be very careful inside that house. The things we can't see can kill us."

Goosebumps rose on my arms. "You're scaring me, Adam."

"I'm warning you, Emma."

I have a vivid imagination, an artist's vision, but after what I'd seen with Mr. Clapp, I felt more like a doubter, a cynic, and already questions were surfacing in my mind. "Why would there be a malevolent spirit in the old Chadwick house in particular? People died at home all the time, and some of the houses date to before the Revolutionary War. There were soldiers here throughout the Civil War. Typhoid and swamp fevers carried off hundreds. Why after those thousands of possibilities would one house, Bev's house, hold an evil ghost?"

Adam looked out over the water. "They were normal people. God-fearing people. But the meanest man who ever lived was a Chadwick. Died in the room where you see the face in the window. His spirit is trapped in that house, and he's not about to relinquish control of his home to living people."

I edged away from him. "You are kidding."

His answer came on a hushed breath. "I wish I were."

"Would you like to try your explanation of Mr. Clapp's attack on the police?"

He smiled then. "They wouldn't believe me any more than you do."

"There's a perfectly rational explanation for Walter Clapp's attack. Another human, maybe someone he knows, tied him up to steal from him. Or did it because he's angry with him, or for revenge or maybe just because he's crazy."

Adam shook his head. "Not this time. He was overpowered by the evil spirit that's trapped in the

Chadwick house. And he'll strike again."

"Who was this mean man whose ghost still roams Chadwick house?"

"Benjamin Chadwick. He killed two men while he was alive, robbed many more, raped at least one woman, drowned another, and destroyed a minister's reputation for fun." Adam's voice held barely contained fury.

This Benjamin Chadwick wouldn't have been a popular man, but how much of this was rumor? Surely, he'd have been in jail if he'd committed all the crimes Adam blamed him for. "How do you know all this?"

"From old man Duffy and tales passed down to him from his grandmother and his mother. From the news reports of the day kept in the library. There was money to be made in this town at the turn of the last century, and it made a man like Benjamin Chadwick greedy and mean. And with money, Benjamin could buy his way out of every difficulty."

"Money? In Summerduck?" While the town was in decent shape now for eastern North Carolina, it was poor when I grew up. Tobacco and cotton had been failing as cash crops, and pigs and chickens hadn't yet taken their place.

"The Chadwicks lived in a boom time for Summerduck. The country needed lumber and there were plenty of forests to cut down. They floated the trees along the rivers to the sawmills. The railroad hauled sawed lumber and farm produce to the west, and boats carried the same products to the cities in the north."

"I can research in the library all day long, and prove everything you say, but I won't find any evidence that a ghost attacked Walter Clapp."

He shook his head. "No, you can't. But it's true."

"Have you ever seen Benjamin Chadwick's ghost?"

"Yes."

"When? How? What did he look like?"

"Like his pictures in the paper. Dark hair, mustache, about my height, muscular build."

That was something I hadn't looked for in the papers. Photos of the Chadwicks. Adam's description sounded like the face in the window, but it could also describe a million other men.

"And the ghost told you who he was?" I was having trouble believing Adam. He didn't sound sane.

"No." His tone said he thought I was being foolish.

"Then how did you know?"

"He looked just like his picture in the papers, and Duffy had seen him before. Knew who he was. Talked to him on occasion."

"Talked to a ghost on occasion?" Now I was having a great deal of trouble believing Adam. If Mr. Duffy were still alive, I wouldn't have believed him, either.

"Scoff if you want. I know what I saw." I couldn't see Adam's face in the shadows from the trees, but his voice was rigid with displeasure.

"Have you always been able to see ghosts?" I wasn't sure I wanted to hear the answer.

"No, and before you ask, he's the only ghost I ever saw."

I was beginning to suspect Adam was off the grid because of mental illness. A suspicion I wouldn't share with anyone. If Mike Randall heard Adam saw ghosts, he'd be looking for Adam to find out if he had attacked Walter Clapp thinking Clapp was a ghost.

Adam faced me for a moment. "I'm trying to protect you. Don't look at me like that, Emma."

"Like what?"

"Like I'm crazy."

"Are you?"

"No." He nearly spit out the word. I was sure I'd hurt his pride.

"Then what I think or how I look at you shouldn't matter."

Adam folded his arms across his chest. Studied the brick walkway. Stared across the river. After a long pause, he said, "It matters because I like you, Emma, and I don't want the evil trapped in that house to attack you. Promise me you won't go back in there."

I liked him too, which made his words more disturbing. Why couldn't I find a nice guy like Adam who wasn't crazy? "I can't do that. For better or worse, it's Bev's house now. She's my friend and she's hired me to coordinate the renovations. I have to go back in there."

"No one ought to go into that house. They ought to set the place on fire. That would solve the problem."

His tone sent shivers along my skin. "Adam, you wouldn't do that, would you?"

"No. God help me, I won't, but it would solve so many

problems."

Oh, yeah. Adam had a mental illness. That was the only explanation. "Solve what problems? Besides the resident ghost, I mean." I reached out to pat his arm.

He shrank back, making sure I didn't touch him. "I'm not crazy, Emma."

"I didn't say you were."

"You were thinking it."

My temper was rising, fueled by Adam's insanity and my desire for him to be sane. "You not only see ghosts, you're also a mind reader?"

"Not everything in life is as black and white as it appears, Emma. I'll see you later." Adam stormed off, disappearing into the darkness before he'd taken a dozen steps.

Chapter Seven

The next day was Sunday. The library and just about everything else in town was closed. If you wanted to see someone, you attended church with them or paid a call after they finished Sunday dinner. Not having anyone I wanted to see, I went to the early service at church, went home to change into shorts, a tank top, and a slathering of sunblock, and then drove to the beach.

I needed to wrap my mind around Adam's mental state. I didn't think he had attacked Mr. Clapp or would burn down the old Chadwick house because he thought an evil spirit lived inside, but I wasn't qualified to make that judgment.

For that matter, Bev said I was far too imaginative. Wouldn't Adam's ability to see ghosts be a form of imagination? Or was his certainty that he saw ghosts a sign of mental problems?

Maybe we had more in common than I thought. After my ex tore my heart into little bits and stomped on it, I went a little mad. Still, I was better now, and even on my worst days, I never saw ghosts.

Perhaps I should be wondering if a ghost could kill a

living person.

I walked for miles through the loose sand. The beach was crowded with people trying to get in one last weekend at the shore before life took on its fall patterns. Happy people. Tanned people. Living people.

Children splashed along the water's edge, seagulls cried out as they swooped in circles on an endless search for food, and a few fishermen drank beer and watched the lines they'd thrown into the surf. I dodged them all as I walked close enough to the water not to burn my feet on the sand.

My muscles ached after a couple of hours of walking, but I still couldn't make up my mind. Was Adam crazy, or did he have an agenda I hadn't spotted? Why would a ghost try to kill a man who'd only been in the house once? Did ghosts dislike certain smells? I walked back to where I'd parked the car, resolved to hit the old newspaper files in the library the next day. At least I could check out the details Adam told me.

Details wouldn't prove Adam was sane. Nothing would prove Adam had or hadn't seen a ghost, but at least I'd know he hadn't made up every inch of his story.

* * *

After a couple more paragraphs written in the same vein about the older generation, I found the first mention of the children. Adam and Benjamin were twenty-five-year-old twins "who were now united in their desire to comfort and protect their younger sister Clarissa." Adam Chadwick "gave a moving eulogy that reminded all present of their great loss since Nathaniel had gone to his reward." Benjamin was not mentioned again.

It wasn't until the next year that I hit pay dirt. Nineteen-year-old Martha Seward, "beloved and beautiful daughter of..."—they then went on to list all her many On my lunch break the next day, I interrupted Dave and his sandwich again. After not-too-patiently checking with his computer, he thumped his cane to the microfiche files and pointed out the drawer holding the local newspaper files for the years 1898 to 1904. "Might as well start with these," he muttered. "They ought to keep you busy for a few days."

"Thanks," I muttered back, already threading a spool onto the machine.

Nathaniel Chadwick, widower, died February 16, 1898, according to that week's local paper. The headline story was the sinking of the *Maine* in Cuba on the fifteenth with the loss of 266 sailors. No doubt it was the deaths of the sailors that made the event front page news. With so many fishermen in the area, we've always been very sensitive to loss of life in a watery grave.

Chadwick's flowery obit mentioned how "he would rejoin the love of his life, his wife Mary," who'd died five years before. The story went on to say "he was buried beside her under a single tombstone in the family plot, united in the ground as all knew they'd been reunited in heaven."

relatives—died by drowning in the Fishhook River. She'd walked to the end of a pier on a moonless night and had accidentally fallen in. An old man living on a barge nearby said he hear a splash and saw a dark figure walk down the pier and away. He described the figure as a ghost walking abroad.

What was it with ghosts in this town?

Martha's body wasn't found until morning when a strong wind from the west forced a great volume of water down river and into the ocean, creating a low wind tide and leaving her body partially exposed in six inches of water on the muddy river bottom. A head wound was attributed to the pier pilings, explaining why a healthy young woman who'd grown up in a river town hadn't cried out or saved herself in an area of shallow water so near the shore.

Two days after that, her funeral had been held. The same day Adam Chadwick had written his final will denying his brother any inheritance.

The next year, the paper carried a story about a mean-spirited rumor attacking the Methodist minister, accusing him of unnatural acts. The next issues mentioned a police investigation, then a story and an editorial on the determination of the police that there was no basis to the rumor.

The paper, in its usual overwrought style, went on about the lack of anyone coming forward to say they had been harmed by the minister. Instead, countless parishioners and citizens were quoted in long, complex sentences saying nearly identical glowing tributes to the minister. Surprisingly for a paper in this time, they even quoted two "negroes," a Baptist minister and a doctor, who gave glowing reports of the Methodist minister's

Christian charity.

Finally, a story ran that the elders of the church had met and the minister had tendered his resignation, which the church accepted with "great sadness and gratefulness for his many fine sermons and acts of kindness to the parishioners. His work among the negro residents of the town would long be remembered by that community."

Benjamin Chadwick's name was never mentioned in these stories. How did Adam, my Adam as I'd come to think of him as opposed to the long dead Adam, know Benjamin Chadwick had a role? Clarissa must have passed the story down to her daughter and grandson, Mr. Duffy, who told Adam.

There'd been a seismic shift in the rights of blacks in the south at the time of these rumors. Until then, African Americans had voted and sat in the state legislature. After that, they were treated as second-class citizens. Had Benjamin been on one side of that issue and this minister on the other? Another question for Adam.

The following year, 1901, the paper ran a story hedged in very circumspect language about a legal case between Anne Harlow, spinster, versus Benjamin Chadwick. For once, the overblown verbiage was set aside in favor of understated vagueness. Chadwick had broken a verbal contract between them and Anne was suing for restitution. Two weeks later, the paper said the court had awarded her monthly support in recompense. I smiled when I saw her lawyer was Adam Chadwick.

On a hunch, I started searching the birth

announcements. Near the end of 1901, I found a few lines saying Anne Harlow had given birth to a boy she named Stephen Chadwick. If my Adam was a descendant of this Stephen Chadwick, no wonder Mr. Duffy would have told him the family history. I needed to find Adam and get these points clarified. Not because I thought a ghost attacked Walter Clapp. Not because anyone from that time would still be alive. I really wasn't sure why these details mattered so much. I just felt they must matter.

I decided Anne Harlow was smart not to marry Benjamin Chadwick when I saw in the following year that Benjamin was arrested for murder.

Over several issues, I read how Marcus Atwell, farmer, was found dead in a field where the ownership was disputed between Atwell and Benjamin Chadwick, the neighboring farmer. The story made clear that the ownership wasn't questioned until Benjamin decided he wanted the land, and he wasn't about to pay for ownership. Having motive and the murder weapon, an axe left at the scene with the initials, NC for Nathaniel Chadwick, burned into the handle, the police arrested Benjamin Chadwick.

The twelve men of Chadwick's jury found him not guilty after his attorney, who was not his brother, produced two witnesses who were with Chadwick from the time Atwell left his house until his body was found by his son an hour later.

The newspaper made clear what type of men these two witnesses were. They "were laborers in the employ of Benjamin Chadwick when they did work, and when they didn't, could be counted on to cause fights, steal trinkets, and drink large quantities of bootleg whiskey."

Sometimes I wished our newspapers today would be so outspoken.

Benjamin and the two men were supposedly in a barn playing cards and drinking "strong spirits" at the time of the attack. One of the jurors was quoted as saying, "the story had the ring of truth to it, even if the speaker didn't."

I didn't find the other murder in the paper, but the rest of the charges Adam laid out against Benjamin Chadwick were possible. Unless his twin brother's death was murder and the motive was the family disagreement. I needed to speak to Adam.

I returned the microfiche to Dave, who was now munching on a bag of chips. As I walked out of the library, I nearly collided with Sergeant Randall. I looked up from the snug T-shirt spread across muscular shoulders to his mirrored sunglasses. "You hang out at the library on your days off?" I asked before my brain stopped my mouth from blurting out the first thought that crossed my mind.

"No. I was looking for you. The shop told me where you were."

I looked at the time on my phone. "And they're probably wondering when I'll finally return from lunch."

I tried to step around him, but he blocked my path. "No, because they know I need your help in finding a suspect. They've given you the time off."

"Me? Who?" And then I knew.

"I want to question your buddy Adam Chadwick."

"Off duty?"

"No one has seen him, although we've been looking. I thought perhaps our uniforms might spook him, so I'm here in civvies."

"You still look like a cop."

He glanced down, arms held out at his sides. "Really?"

His sneakers and jeans were worn, so they weren't a giveaway. "We can't do anything about your haircut or your build, but at least lose the shades."

He took them off and I found myself staring into gorgeous dark blue eyes with long eyelashes. He had chiseled cheekbones to match his strong jaw. When I finally blinked, I realized I'd been lost in his gaze. He turned and watched a car drive slowly between the two rows of parked cars.

I took in a deep breath. Randall was a jerk, but he was a lean muscled package of beautiful jerk. "What crime is Adam suspected of committing?"

"Attacking Mr. Clapp."

"He said he didn't want the police involved. That it was an accident."

"Gary Lofton convinced him otherwise."

That creep. I took a deep breath and let it out. "Where shall we look for Adam?"

"Thought we'd start with the old Chadwick place while you tell me what you know about him."

When I started to walk down the street, he took my arm and led me to a non-descript white pickup truck. One look at the storm clouds building overhead and I was glad we'd have cover in case of a sudden thunderstorm. He opened the door for me and I grabbed a handle on the door column while I planted one foot on the floorboard to swing myself up into the passenger seat of the cab. Once seated, I realized Randall would have a good view of traffic over other vehicles. While he blocked the view for little hatchbacks like mine.

He shut the door and walked around the front while I did a quick inspection of the interior. Clean, no trash, with an impressive two-way radio mounted on the dashboard.

Once he was inside, he started up the engine to turn on the air conditioning and then faced me. "Okay, what's this guy's story? Is he crazy or slow?"

"He's certainly not slow."

"Then he's crazy."

If I told Randall about the evil spirit in the Chadwick house, he'd definitely put Adam down as crazy. And maybe me, too. "I don't think so."

"But?"

"I didn't say 'but.'"

"You didn't have to. You were thinking it."

"No, I wasn't." Even I didn't believe I sounded convincing.

He smiled and aimed those gorgeous eyes at me. "Sugarbear, you're a smart girl. Your antennae have to be going off about this guy. No address, no record, no history, no friends. What's his connection to that house?"

"I found out one of the Chadwicks had an illegitimate son in 1901. I think perhaps Adam is a descendant."

"Did he say so?"

"No."

"Why not?"

"Embarrassment? Or maybe he's curious about where his family came from but doesn't want anyone to know he's following up on the skeleton in the family closet."

Mike gave me his *get real* look. "He could still be our attacker."

"Why would he harm an exterminator working in the house? He'd know this was just a person hired by Bev. He didn't need to worry about being caught inside."

"Robbery. Revenge. The guy has no obvious means of support. He does have a history, probably under another name. He could have a history with Clapp. Perhaps Clapp recognized him and threatened to expose him."

"Did Mr. Clapp say so?"

A grumble was Mike's only answer.

"So, you're chasing a theory."

"Only until we catch Chadwick and ask him." The mischievous grin I remembered from elementary school flashed for an instant. Mike put the truck into gear and drove the few blocks to the Chadwick house. He parked across the street and looked around. "Here's where you get out, Sugarbear."

"And you?"

"I'll wait here until he shows up."

"You're using me as bait?" He couldn't get much more insulting.

"Yeah. Go on."

Furious, I slid off the seat and slammed the truck door. The panel truck parked in front of the house told me some workmen were around, either inside or out. They were on the left-hand side, taking down their ladders as they glanced at the storm clouds. I could see where they'd begun painting and replacing boards. "Looks good so far," I told them.

"Yeah. It's going to take a while," the older man said.

"Has there been a man around here today? Blondish hair, a little taller than me?"

"I haven't seen anyone. You, Matt?"

The younger painter shook his head. They passed me as they carried one of the ladders around to the street.

I walked into the backyard to find Adam standing by the barn or garage or shed or whatever the tumbledown structure was. "Hey, somebody wants to meet you."

His expression wasn't welcoming. "What if I don't want to meet them?"

I stopped two feet in front of him. "He thinks you attacked Mr. Clapp."

"I didn't."

"Then you need to meet him and tell him so." I moved a little closer and held out a hand. "I read up on the stories you told me about in the newspaper. If Benjamin Chadwick was behind all those deaths and rumors and what-have-you, he was a dangerous man."

"He was, and he was. And his spirit is trapped in that house. He's killed before, and he'll kill again."

An idea came to me. "Has his ghost ever killed

before?"

"No. The house was in his family. He didn't need to. They wouldn't bother him."

I pressed on. "Are you Benjamin's descendant?"

He drew back, blinking. "Why would you say that?"

"Benjamin had an illegitimate son, Stephen. Are you his descendant?"

He scowled at me. "No."

"Did Mr. Duffy think you were? Is that why he told you the family stories?"

"Duffy was a lonely old man. I'd sit on his porch with him sometimes, and he'd talk. That's how I knew about the family."

I was so focused on Adam, I didn't notice Mike coming toward us until he was almost there. Adam must have seen my surprise and turned around. One instant he was there, the next he dashed into one side of the shed.

Mike crossed the last few yards and ran into the shed an instant behind Adam. I heard some crashing sounds and a yelp, and then Mike appeared at the far end of the shed rubbing his arm. "Did he come by you?"

"No." I was surprised not to see Adam in Mike's grip.

"Sugarbear, don't lie to me," he growled.

"I'm not."

He stalked up to me, fury in his eyes. "Just past the far side of the shed is a tall brick wall around the house on the next street. He couldn't have scaled it that fast, and no one can walk through a solid brick wall. He had to have come out one side of the shed or the other, and he didn't get past me. Which way did he go?"

I folded my arms over my chest and held my ground as best I could. "He didn't come out into the yard and there's no place to hide now that Bev's had everything chopped down. He had to have jumped over the wall."

"Only if he can fly." He scowled as he leaned over me. "You know the penalties for aiding and abetting a fugitive."

"He can't be a fugitive because there's no arrest warrant for him." Despite knowing I was right, I wanted to back away from Randall. He was one intimidating creep when he wanted to be.

"Come on. Let's circle the block. See if we can find him." Sergeant Randall walked away, not checking to see if I followed.

The first fat raindrops that hit my head assured I was right behind him.

Chapter Eight

Randall circled a few blocks in the tightly packed historic neighborhood without either of us spotting Adam. I told him Adam denied being an illegitimate descendent. Grumbling, the police sergeant dropped me off at the art supply/stationery shop as the cloudburst slowed to a mist.

As soon as I walked in, my boss said, "The clerk of the court called. We need to take these supplies up to the courthouse immediately. Before you get settled, run them up there, will you?" She set a filled cardboard box on the counter and walked away, certain I'd do what she wanted.

People were taking me for granted that afternoon and I was beginning to get annoyed. This wasn't the first time I'd run supplies to the courthouse when they discovered a sudden need in a courtroom or board room, but before that day I had volunteered.

Fortunately, the rain had stopped.

I could walk beneath the Spanish moss to the courthouse without drowning. The rain had washed the city smells from the air, replacing it with humidity you could cut with a knife. I hurried so I could get back into air conditioning.

The courthouse was a massive two-story red brick Queen Anne building with black wrought iron trim and an imposing staircase leading up to the front door on the first floor. Modern sensibilities had added a handicapped access to the basement and an elevator.

As I entered the courthouse lobby, I met up with my fire chief landlord. "In budget talks?" I asked.

Bobby nodded ruefully.

"If you want, I'll go in and tell the aldermen that you're worth every penny you're asking for. And I have ways to get people's attention."

He burst out laughing, the sound dissolving in the old high-ceilinged area. People turned and looked, saw it was Bobby, and smiled.

He'd heard the call the night I dropped by the bar to see my then husband, my purse stuffed with the evidence of several of his recent liaisons. You'd think my sneaky ex would have had enough sense not to bring his explicit love letters and even more explicit photos home. When I confronted the cheating creep and demanded he destroy his trophies, he refused. Then he laughed. That's when I lit the matches and began burning the letters and photos in the middle of the bar.

Bobby had run in with the first truck after the fire alarms and sprinklers went off. I ran behind the bar, grabbed the first tool at hand, an axe, and took off after my cheating spouse. It was Bobby, not the police, who had disarmed me. He'd listened without making any judgment and then walked me to the police cruiser. Really, he was helping the cops, but he did it with old-fashioned southern charm.

Unfortunately, my slime ball ex charged me with assault. That led to my commitment in a psych ward.

The only place in the entire town where I can't be called Psycho-babe is in Bobby's hearing.

"I've heard there's been a problem at the house the Myers's bought." Bobby would have heard more about Walter Clapp's assault than I knew, but that was his subtle permission for me to tell him about it if I wanted.

"I found Mr. Clapp very neatly tied up. Terrible way to start a weekend." Then I realized how my words sounded. "For him and for us."

"You doin' okay?"

"Yeah. Thanks. Good luck with the budget." I gave him a smile and set off toward the clerk of court's office.

Mission accomplished, I started back to the shop when my cell phone rang. "Hello?"

"Emma? It's Bev. Trouble at the house. Can you get over there now?"

"I'll meet you there." After calling the shop and reporting I'd accomplished my task and would be back in the morning, I trotted the few blocks to the old Chadwick place. The painters and carpenters were all in the front yard.

One of them, I guessed the foreman, came over to me. Sweat slid down his tanned skin. "You're that friend of Mrs. Myers, aren't ya? Well, she better get here soon, 'cause we're leaving."

"What happened?"

"Damned house tried to kill Bud."

I guessed Bud was the young man with the ripped T-shirt, torn jeans, and bloody arm. A quick look told me the damage to his clothing preceded his injuries. I raised my eyebrows. "How did the house try to kill him? By putting him in a clothing shredder?"

"That's just Bud." The foreman waved in Bud's direction like he was shooing a pesky fly. "The house dropped a ladder on him. If he hadn't heard it slide, it would'a landed smack on his head."

"Perhaps he should have put it up more carefully."

"There was nothing wrong with how that ladder was set," he snapped at me.

I tried to sound reasonable. "This yard isn't exactly smooth. Maybe he got one leg caught in a hole."

"Inside the house? It was set up across that bathroom from where Bud was framing out a wall. And this isn't the first incident. Every time we go to work inside, something goes wrong."

"And nothing happens when you work outside?"

"No."

He was either crazy, pulling my leg, or angling for more money from Bev. "Then I'd suggest working on the outside until we find a cause for your accidents."

He glanced up at the storm clouds that were building again. "No sense setting up again today. We'll be back tomorrow, but we'll only work on the outside."

"With a price that reflects the outside work only."

"Hey. We've bought the inside paint and caulking, framing lumber and sheet rock. It's already on site. The bill will show that, too."

I muttered "No doubt" as Bev came across the yard toward us, her paint-splattered smock flapping open with each quick step.

"What is this all about?" she asked, hands on hips as she stood in front of the foreman.

"Bud went to work inside. A ladder crossed the room and tried to brain him."

I glanced back at the young man and wondered if the ladder had tried to hit him in the crotch. I doubted a blow to his skull would register in his thought processes.

The foreman kept up his stream of complaints, ending with, "This isn't the first time strange things have happened in there. We're not working inside again."

"We have an agreement," Bev said. "Tell him, Emma. We have an agreement."

"You have an agreement with the owner, Mr. Scott," I told Bev. "I'd tell him this crew refuses to honor the agreement. Maybe he has another crew that isn't accident prone." I gave the foreman a false smile.

He glared at me. "These aren't accidents."

"Your crew is deliberately doing this to themselves?"

"No. How can you say that? Something is knocking ladders over and tripping my men. Boards fly up and strike them in the back. That house is dangerous."

"Who's going to believe that?" Bev said.

I had to back Bev, but I was thinking about the evil

spirit Adam told me lived in that house. What if he was right? I took a deep breath to shake off my doubts and said, "Has anyone seen the boards or the ladder flying through the air on their own? Any witnesses to these strange happenings?"

The foreman's face took on a mulish expression, but he didn't say a word.

"I didn't think so. Either one of your men is a practical joker, or the crew has been careless and won't admit it."

"We'll work on the outside while you get an electrician to rewire the inside. Maybe that'll clear up the problem." The foreman walked away to a rumble of thunder. His crew, who'd been packing up while we talked, hopped into their trucks.

"I guess that's what I'll have to do. Who knew tradesmen were so superstitious," Bev said. I noticed her fists hadn't left her hips.

The trucks roared to life and drove slowly off under the canopy of ancient trees. We stood and watched them roll away.

I glanced around, but Adam was not in sight. Sergeant Randall must have scared him off. "Let me know when you want me back to help. I'm going home before I get caught in the rain."

Bev started back in the same direction. For the first time, I had a chance to notice the bright blue paint in her dark hair. It looked nice.

"Is there an old superstition about the house being

haunted?" I asked as we hurried along.

"It's those two deaths. One in the barn or shed or whatever, and then the other in the house a few days later. They were both young men, and the house stayed in the family until now. Old man Duffy had been, well, odd for the past ten years before his death. That just added to the rumors about the house."

"So, it's the house that's normal and the residents who are cracked?" I asked and then smiled at Bev.

"Careful," she warned with an answering smile. "We own it now."

"Like I said...," I began as the rain started to fall and another blast of thunder rolled through the neighborhood.

"Very funny," Bev said as she began to jog down the street toward her home.

* * *

It was two days later before I got another distress call from Bev, asking me to meet her at lunchtime at the Chadwick house while she talked to an electrician. She promised quiche, fresh fruit, and sweet tea. I said I'd meet her. I'm easy.

They were on the back porch standing near the fuse box when I arrived. "We'll need to put a new fuse panel inside the house. Where would you like it?" Mr. Ellery, the electrician asked.

Bev chose the pantry that would become her laundry room with only five minutes of dithering. Meanwhile, my stomach grumbled with hunger. I could see another issue, which would probably postpone my lunch even longer.

"The current electrical lines are run along the baseboards because these are old-fashioned lathe and plaster walls. Do you plan to do the same thing except where they're going to remodel the kitchen and baths?" I asked.

"It would be easier and cheaper," Mr. Ellery said.

Bev made a puzzled, squinting face and an "aaaah" noise. "I'm not sure."

"I'll work the estimate up both ways, so you can see how large a difference it'll make."

"Okay. Let's see the rest of the house," Bev said cheerfully. I didn't want to be around when she and Roger decided on that estimate. Roger's financial restraint and Bev's dreamy plans were already colliding over this house. When Bev told me, I didn't have the heart to say it would only get worse.

Fortunately, they had a solid marriage. Not like my union with my serial cheater. Oh, I was glad I was rid of him. And it had only taken me a few months with a shrink to figure it out.

I followed them around while Ellery measured and wrote on his clipboard.

"What if we want to put ceiling fans in?"

"Let me know which rooms, and I can figure in the cost running the wire both inside and outside the walls."

Their conversation went like that while my stomach grumbled and I kept thinking about the quiche waiting for me. Finally, he'd seen everything, made a few more notes, and left. I hurried to pull lunch out of the creaky old refrigerator while Bev walked him off the back porch and said goodbye.

It was my voice that grumbled when Bev returned with Mrs. Doris Carmichael, chair of the Historical Society. The older woman looked around with a critical sniff. At least she wasn't wearing her red rubber boots.

"You are painting this house an unapproved color," she began. "All exterior changes must be approved by my committee."

"Then it's a good thing no one has started painting anything yet," I shot back. "So far, the workmen have been replacing boards and priming wood due to the lack of maintenance allowed by your committee over a number of years."

"We didn't judge Mr. Duffy capable of making repairs." Her pinkish-white helmet of hair shimmied in displeasure at my statement.

"May I quote you on that? Because if you use that as your defense in court, the judge will disband your committee and replace it with something under town jurisdiction." I knew nothing of the sort, but between the divorce and the commitment hearings, I'd spent enough time around lawyers to spout some ominous sounding legalese.

"Our aim is to keep the neighborhood looking its best."

"By letting this house fall apart, and then questioning every move we make when we try to make it habitable?" Bev asked, her arms crossed over her chest.

"So far you haven't made any progress. When can we expect to see changes?" Mrs. Carmichael countered.

"Are you going to criticize or demand changes to those efforts?" I asked.

"I won't know until I see them."

"What about the rest of your committee? Do they need to see them, too?"

"Of course."

"You're looking for a lawsuit, aren't you Mrs. Carmichael?" I asked.

"Of course not."

"You've come around here, threatening the owner by saying she's having the house painted an unapproved color, while you've not produced a list of approved colors by manufacturer. You can be sure all of this is being noted." I gave her a frosty smile.

"We've never made such a list, finding it too confining when color names change all the time."

"Then the house couldn't be painted an approved color. You've made it impossible for this owner, or any owner, to comply."

"Just bring a paint sample of any exterior paints you plan to use to the next committee meeting so we can approve them." She was nearly spitting her words at me.

My smile broadened. "Wouldn't it have been easier to begin by saying that?"

She turned to face Bev. "Thank you, Mrs. Myers. We'll see you at the library tomorrow afternoon at three with the paint samples."

Out of the corner of my eye, I saw a gallon of paint slide across the floor. On its flat bottom rather than rolling. An impossible trick. It didn't make a sound as it skimmed over the floor boards, heading for Mrs. Carmichael's feet.

"Watch out!" I cried as I leaped forward, grabbing for the older woman as she turned, caught her foot on the full paint can, and started to teeter.

She windmilled her arms, clipping Bev on the shoulder with one hand while I clutched her bony waist and kept her upright. When she'd regained her balance, she glared into my face. I let her go. She then peered down and stepped carefully around the can, all the time frowning. "You should be careful where you leave construction material. Anyone could get hurt."

"Not if they watch where they're going," Bev said, rubbing her shoulder.

"I'd expect anyone setting foot in a construction site to be smart enough to watch their step. Otherwise, they have no business being here," I said, knowing full well Mrs. Carmichael's accident would have been one for the record books. Paint cans don't move themselves silently across the room. Certainly not on a flat surface.

Yet one had here, aimed at the one person who could stop the repairs on this house faster than anyone else in town. Adam had called the spirit of this house malevolent. Perhaps the goal of the ghost of Benjamin Chadwick was to stop our work. He didn't want his house altered.

We escorted Mrs. Carmichael outside, down the front steps of the house and past the painters and carpenters working on the exterior. At least we made it to the sidewalk without any additional strange occurrences.

Finally, we could go inside and eat our quiche in peace. I knew I should tell Bev what I saw, but I doubted she'd believe me. She was too busy describing the draperies she planned for various windows to notice that I barely said a word.

I hardly believed what I'd seen. How could I expect anyone else to trust my story?

Suddenly, I had no appetite for lunch.

Chapter Nine

As soon as we finished eating, or in my case breaking my quiche into crumbs, I said I had to get back to the shop and rushed out of the house. The creepy feeling making my skin itch hadn't left me since I'd seen the paint can glide across the floor. If I hadn't intervened, Mrs. Carmichael would definitely have tripped and fallen.

Why would a malevolent spirit attack Mrs. Carmichael? Ruling out the possibility the old woman had the same effect on ghosts that she had on me, I could only see one reason. The spirit wanted the Historical Society to throw as many roadblocks in Bev's way as possible so the house would be unchanged. Unlived in. Dilapidated.

The phantom apparently considered the house as his property and didn't want to share. That was believable, but how would I convince Bev the spirit was there? Worse, the bank wouldn't let the Myers out of their mortgage for a little thing like vicious ghosts who wouldn't leave.

That thought brought me back to Walter Clapp's assault and Adam's contention that a ghost was the culprit. I needed to talk to Adam and find out if there was any way to make the spirit depart.

I rounded a corner and found Adam leaning against an ancient oak. "How did you know I was looking for you?" I asked.

He gave me a heart-stopping smile. "I didn't. I was looking for you."

I stared at him, trying to decide if I'd tell him what I'd seen in the Chadwick house.

His expression turned serious. "You've seen him, haven't you?"

I shook my head. It didn't lessen the tension growing in my neck or the fear that I was going mad. "I saw a paint can glide across the floor and stop where a little old lady would trip over it."

"Was she hurt?"

"No. I called out and caught her before she fell."

"What reason would the ghost have for tripping up an old lady?" Adam asked me.

"I don't know. He's your ghost," I snapped back. Seeing the hurt look on his face, I relented. "She's the head of the Historical Society. She thinks she has the final say on any changes my friends make to their new home. The Chadwick house."

"Does she? Have the final say?"

"No, but no one is willing to ignore her input. The society is politically powerful in town and she runs the society."

"So, you have to stay in her good graces. If she'd tripped over that paint can, she would have made it harder for your friends to make any repairs on the house."

I nodded. "The painters are already refusing to work inside the house. A ladder supposedly moved across a room to fall on one of the workmen."

"In other words, the malevolent spirit in the house has been busy."

"It's not funny, Adam."

"I know it's not. Want to go walk along the river?"

I looked between the trees at the dark clouds billowing overhead. "I have to get back to the shop, and I'd like to get there before it rains."

"Then I should let you get on your way." He turned away, then swung back to face me. "Perhaps your friends would be safer if they tore the house down and built again."

"The Historical Society would never allow it. Besides, Bev and Roger love that house. They have plans for every inch of the building. New plumbing, electric, heating and cooling, appliances, a home office for Roger, a state-of-the-art kitchen for Bev, a home theater room. Everything they want mixed in with all the antiques they've collected." Bev's enthusiasm for the house came through in my voice. Since I couldn't afford to do anything like this myself, I guess I'd been living my fantasies through Bev.

"I guess people with dreams don't take the safe route. Take care, Emma. I'll see you later." With a wave, Adam walked past me and away.

I wondered where he was going for just an instant. Then, a clap of thunder shook the sky and I hurried on before I got drenched.

I made it as far as the library before the skies opened up. I ran inside and headed to Dave's desk. For once, I hadn't interrupted his lunch. "Is there a book of pictures of the leading families in town in about 1900?" I asked.

"There is a book of old photos, with pictures of local dignitaries mixed in with other photos of the time." He rose, thumping his cane as he led me to another room and studied a bookshelf. Finally, he put his hand on an old leather hardbound volume and pulled it out.

I spent a fascinated hour studying old photos of houses, horses, early autos, sailboats, barges, and trolleys, some of them including people. Near the back of the book, I found a picture of the old Chadwick house when it was new. On the front porch were five people.

I borrowed a magnifying glass from Dave and studied the photo. There was a bearded man, identified as Nathaniel Chadwick, standing next to a shorter woman who was his wife. The young girl standing near her parents was labeled as Clarissa.

Two young men, perhaps in their early twenties, one blondish and the other dark, stood on opposite sides of the porch. Perhaps it was a trick of the magnifying glass, but they appeared to be staring angrily at each other.

The darker one was identified as Benjamin and looked like a younger version of the face in the window. The lighter one was labeled Adam.

He looked like the Adam Chadwick I knew at a younger age. Despite his denials, Adam had to be related to the Chadwicks who lived in that house.

* * *

My cell phone rang just as I walked through the front door after work, soaked from the most recent storm that had opened up the heavens a block from my house. Although my second-floor apartment has a separate entrance off the wide front porch and she'd never see it, I knew Bobby's wife, Aunt Jean, wouldn't want me to drip on her hardwood floors.

I stood on the throw rug and answered the phone, careful to keep all the drops on the carpet. "Hello?"

"There you are, Sugarbear. How about some dinner?" Mike Randall's voice snapped out of the phone at me as a command.

"You're asking me out for dinner?" Dating Sergeant Randall was low on my list of things I wanted to do. On the other hand, dinner was dinner.

"Yeah. I want to talk to you. Taking you out to dinner seems like a nice way to carry on a conversation."

He'd always been direct. I looked at the ceiling for inspiration. Nothing. "Where are you taking me?"

"I thought the Cannon."

He knew I couldn't resist good seafood, and the Cannon had the best in town. "What time?"

"I'll pick you up in half an hour."

Before I could agree, he clicked off the call. There was nothing wrong with Mike's ego.

I was ready and almost to the door exactly a half hour later when he hammered on my door with his fist. Hearing his knock, I opened the door expecting to have him serve me with a search warrant.

Instead, he smiled and said, "Ready?"

Holding a golf umbrella over us, he walked me the few blocks to the Cannon Restaurant overlooking the Fishhook River. There actually were Civil War cannons facing the river in the park next door to the restaurant. Any student of history in Summerduck will tell you the town was overrun by Yankees without the cannons firing a shot. The Union Army invaded across the shallow Wales River on the south side of town, rendering the cannons useless.

The Cannon served great seafood without bothering about ambiance. I'd stood close enough to Mike under the umbrella; I didn't need him thinking a fancy restaurant left me in his debt. Ordering off the plastic menus went well. I ordered the shrimp plate with baked potato and green beans and asked for cocktail sauce rather than tartar sauce. Mike ordered the large fish plate.

I kept waiting for the reason I would regret this dinner.

We clinked iced tea glasses and then Mike said, "Have you seen Chadwick lately?"

O-kay. "I knew there was a reason for this dinner."

"Couldn't you think it was for the pleasure of your company?"

"No."

"I know you won't go home with me tonight—"

I growled at the suggestion. Mike only saw women two ways. Proper married women and mothers who deserved respect, and young women who were good for one thing. Since I was again single, I fell into the second category.

"—and I wanted some return on my investment, so I decided to ask you about Chadwick."

Dinner as an investment? My blood sizzled, and not in a good way. "You'd make a much better impression if you weren't so blatant."

"Everybody wants something. Even your friend Chadwick. I'm just honest about what I want."

"Fine. I'll be honest, too. I saw him this afternoon for a minute or two while I was returning to work from the Chadwick house."

"Where, exactly?"

I told him the names of the streets at that intersection.

"Did you tell him we wanted to talk to him?"

"No."

"Why not, Em? It's not like we're planning to throw him into a dungeon."

I shook my head. "We were talking about something else."

"What?"

I took refuge in my iced tea.

"Come on, baby doll. What were you two talking about?"

Our appetizers came. I dug in to the calamari.

He gave me a minute and then said, "Sugarbear, I want an answer."

I leaned back in my chair and said, "You'll never

believe me."

"Try me."

"You'll think we're crazy." I corrected that. "You'll think I'm crazy."

"Maybe." He didn't smile when he said that. Did he think I still had one foot in the psych ward? "But you'll never know until you tell me."

I looked at him intently. "Do you believe in ghosts?"

His answer was a booming laugh.

"Well, I have my answer."

When he finally stopped laughing, he said, "Emma, you're not exactly the type to believe in ghosts."

"And what type am I?" The cold anger in my voice would have warned off a smarter man.

Mike plunged ahead. "Down to earth. Sensible. Not all woo-woo and Ouija boards. Look at you, Sugarbear. You're wearing a nice black dress and flats. A girl who believes in ghosts would wear lots of gauzy fabric and clunky sandals."

There was no point in explaining to Sergeant Mike Randall that people change and frequently are not what they appear. That criminals can turn their lives around. That a pillar of the community can hide a dark secret. That I could be changing my mind about ghosts.

"Forget it, Mike. Forget I said anything at all." I tossed my napkin on the table and moved to rise.

He held up his hand. "Whoa. Wait. Okay. We won't talk about Chadwick or ghosts. Tell me how the work is going at the Myers' house."

"Badly. The painters have been experiencing a lot of minor accidents they can't explain, but only inside the house. They won't go back in until the electricians get their work done."

"Bad luck for the Myers. Maybe the electricians will be more dependable."

"Maybe," I replied. And maybe they'd be scared off by the evil spirit lurking in that house.

Our dinners came, smelling of Old Bay and lemon. We both began to eat, letting our disagreement fade for a few minutes.

When Mike was nearly finished, he asked, "What does your friend Chadwick say about these accidents?"

I decided to tell him. "He believes they're caused by an evil spirit that resides in the house."

Chuckling, he shook his head. "How did an evil spirit come to land in the Chadwick house?"

"A man died in the house in 1904. A very bad man. His name was Benjamin Chadwick and he killed several people, according to Chadwick family stories."

"He killed them as a ghost or while he was alive?"

"While he was alive. He admitted killing his brother but claimed self-defense. He was tried in another murder but was acquitted because of an alibi provided by two men in his employ who were described as untrustworthy. Old man Duffy supposedly told Adam that his grandmother told him this long-dead Chadwick also drowned a young lady and destroyed another man's reputation."

"And because of these old family stories, your buddy

Chadwick claims Walter Clapp was attacked by a ghost? And the painters have been frightened off by a ghost?"

"Yes."

A booming laugh was his answer.

I was only half-finished with my dinner, but my fork and my napkin landed on the table before I folded my arms over my chest. "Don't laugh. The houses in the old part of town are full of ghosts."

"Ghost stories for the tourists and to keep children in line. Remember? We used to love those stories when we were in school. But they're not real, Sugarbear."

"Not all of them, certainly. But there are unexplained phenomena associated with some of the houses. Noises, objects moving, illusions."

"Phenomena caused by alcohol, drugs, and insanity." Suddenly, instead of sounding like my old school friend, he sounded like a cop.

"Not all of them, Mike." I put out a hand and touched his arm. "I saw a paint can move across the floor in Bev's house today."

He looked stunned for an instant, the expression disappearing from his face so quickly I barely glimpsed his shock. "I don't believe it. You, Sugarbear?"

"Yes, me. I couldn't believe it myself. I still don't. But the paint can started in one place and ended up across the room."

"Bev or a workman moved it while you weren't looking."

I shook my head. "No. I saw it move. And it didn't roll.

It slid on the flat bottom of the can."

"Have you had any hallucinations before? When you were—ill?"

The look I gave him should have burned him to ash. "Don't be so condescending. I've never had hallucinations. My problem was impulse control and depression."

He took my hand and stared into my face. Without his shades, he had beautiful eyes. "The land around here is unsteady. Everything's built on sand. They've been doing work around that house, moving equipment, stuff like that. The ground shifted a little, causing the house to lean just enough that the can slid."

"Do you think so?"

"I know so. Somebody digs a well, takes water from the water table, and the sand above shifts. The effects can travel for miles underground."

I nodded. He was right. "But the can ended up right behind Mrs. Carmichael from the Historical Society. She nearly tripped over it."

He bit back a smile. "I had to deal with her a few times as a patrol officer. Is she still as charming as she was then?"

"Charming isn't the word I'd use."

"Isn't the word I'd use either, but I'm trying to learn to be diplomatic. The chief's demanding it."

I silently wished the Chief of Police good luck with that. "She hasn't changed."

"She probably tripped and tried to blame the Myers or the workmen, when it was her own clumsiness." He nodded, satisfied with his conclusion.

"She did, but the can moved on its own. I saw it. She didn't."

"The ground shifted. Probably the reason for the painters' accidents, too. Maybe the Myers ought to have someone check to make sure the house isn't sitting on some fault line caused by digging wells or construction."

"Oh, they do not want me to suggest that."

He grinned. "Those old houses are money pits. Just keep that in mind if the trouble continues."

"An exorcism would be easier."

"If you have one of those, can I come watch?"

Seeing his eager face and hearing the thrill in his voice, I knew he was serious. I guessed there was less excitement in small town policing than I expected if someone who didn't believe in ghosts wanted to see them driven out. Or maybe he just craved a new and unusual experience. "I'll let you know."

"You want dessert?"

"No thanks."

Randall walked me home through the drizzle. Neither of us said much, probably because neither of us was satisfied with the way the conversation had gone. Randall's suggestion that the house was shifting because of the ground underneath didn't feel right to me. I knew what I saw. Plus, the foundation had just been rebuilt, which should have made the house steadier. The only problem now was how to prove the cause of these accidents.

I walked upstairs to my apartment and sat down

hard on my sofa as I realized what I wanted. Proof that something I didn't believe in existed.

Chapter Ten

Trouble didn't return to the old Chadwick place until Monday. By noon, an electrician had been shocked putting in a new 220 line that had never been hooked up to a power source, and the painters found some problems with the roof. Bev was on the phone to the shop, demanding my presence on my lunch hour. She sweetened the offer with turkey and avocado subs and sweet tea.

When I arrived, I found Bev by the back steps with Mr. Ellery of Ellery Electrical. She spotted me and waved in my direction. "Would you please tell her what you told me?"

"Charlie got a nasty shock installing the 220 line. It wasn't charged."

"Static electricity?" I asked, knowing that didn't happen in our hot and humid summers. It took dry air to create enough static electricity to notice.

"No. It was more than that. What is with this house? We've been hearing rumors." Ellery studied the house as if expecting it to speak or dance at any moment.

I shrugged. "Bad luck. Bad karma. Clumsy painters

trying to hide their goofs. Shifting water table under the house causing the ground to settle. I don't know."

"Whatever it is, I'll tell you, Miz Myers, I got a bad feeling."

"Tell Charlie I hope he feels better. Work in pairs if it'll make you feel better about being in the house. Maybe that way, you'll discover what's causing these strange happenings." Bev was good at soothing troubled nerves.

"Or maybe we don't want to find out what's causing them." He shrugged. "Yeah, we'll give that a try, but it'll cost you extra."

"As long as it's not too much extra. My husband is losing patience." Bev's shoulders slumped as she breathed out.

I knew how much the house meant to her. I wanted to kick the foundation. Or the ghost.

"We'll start after lunch. I hope to have the new panel in today," Ellery said as he walked off.

Only then could I ask Bev, "What about the roof?"

"We knew we had problems there, but the roofers can't start for a few days. Right now, that's the least of my problems."

"What's wrong, Bev?"

"What isn't wrong?" Tears slid down her cheeks. "Roger wants to forget the whole thing. Finish the repairs to the outside and resell the house for whatever we can get."

I gave her a hug. "Hang in there. I think I know someone who might be able to help. Now, you promised me lunch. I'm famished."

We went inside and sat at the table and chairs Bev had set up in the kitchen. The room was so big, and there were so few appliances and counters taking up space that the new furniture looked tiny and fragile in the middle of the room.

Once she'd taken a few bites of her sub, Bev said, "Who is this friend, and how can he help?"

"I'm not going to say any more until I find out exactly what he knows. He may not be able to help, but it's worth a try. Let me finish lunch and I'll see if I can reach him."

Despite Bev's best attempts, I wouldn't tell her anything about Adam or what he'd told me. I wasn't sure I could convince him to meet Bev and tell her about the stories he'd heard from old Mr. Duffy. I didn't relish the idea of telling Bev about a ghost in her house without my source of information on all things Chadwick.

I walked out the back door and around the house, hoping Adam would appear at any time. I circled the block. I walked along the opposite side of the street where I'd first spoken to him. There were people out—dog walkers, workmen, gardeners working in their yards—but no Adam.

Deciding he must have found casual labor for the day, I headed back to the shop.

I left work late that day, having made up some of my missed hours so my paycheck wouldn't be too puny, and walked home by way of the riverbank. The wide river was gray, reflecting the black towering storm clouds, and the wind worked up whitecaps. No boats were out on the choppy water. No insects braved the gusts. The weather felt wild and dangerous. The cool air buffeting my skin spoke to the adventurer in me.

Adam stood on the walkway watching me approach. I thought at first he looked angry, but as I got closer, I could see he looked sad.

"What's wrong?" I asked as soon as I reached him.

"You looked so determined to find me. I can only guess it has to do with the evil inside your friends' house."

"How do you know I'm determined to find you?" He was getting the impression I was looking for him every time we met. It was true, but I don't need a guy thinking I'm that desperate for him.

"I don't. I guess I just wanted to see you, Emma."

The honesty I detected in his voice prompted me to respond in kind. "You were right. I wanted to see you, too. And not just because of the house."

The wind picked up, tossing trash and leaves down the street. The trees bowed and twisted. We'd soon get hit with another thunderstorm.

He stood very close and stared into my eyes. "I want you to know, no matter what happens, that I've never felt a closeness to a woman as I have to you." His smile was sorrowful. "I'm glad you like me, too."

My stomach tightened with my fear of revealing the truth as I moved closer to him to make my admission. "I've never met a man like you. I'm not sure what to make of you, Adam. It's like you can read my mind. You know what makes everyone tick."

"I've had a lot of practice. That's why I know you're so special."

At that moment, the heavens opened up. It took me a moment to open my umbrella. Once I did, I looked around and Adam was gone. "Adam?"

"I'm here."

I blinked. Adam still stood in front of me, a transparent version of him, so transparent I'd missed him the first time I looked.

I could see raindrops splashing off the sidewalk and the waves on the gray river by staring through Adam. But a faint image of Adam was still in front of me. "Adam?"

"Don't be frightened, Emma. I'm still here." His voice was unchanged.

"What happened?" If I'd looked up without my umbrella, I'd have drowned. My mouth hung open in growing confusion and terror. He'd all but disappeared in the rain. People don't do that.

He hung his head. When he raised it again, his expression was as sad as any I'd ever seen. Odd, since he was nothing more than an impression. I shouldn't have been able to see his expression and see the river through him, but I could. "I'm a ghost, Emma. I'm the ghost of Adam Chadwick, who was murdered in 1904 by my brother, Benjamin."

I felt like someone slammed their fist into my sternum. "No. You can't be. You make me smile. You make me believe men can be kind and gentle. I want you to be real. Alive. Please. I want you to be part of my life." I was begging, and for once I didn't care.

"I want to be alive. I want to touch your hand, but I can't. Oh, Emma, forgive me. If I could come back to life, it would be for the pleasure of holding you."

I looked down at my hands and said, "I must be hallucinating. I've been out in the rain too long." I hurried forward, toward my house, toward safety. The rain had nothing on the tears flowing down my cheeks.

The specter that was Adam stepped out of my way. "This must be so hard for you, Emma. You've never seen any of us before, have you?"

"No. Because you don't exist. You can't be dead." I kept rushing forward through the rain, wanting to return to a time before the storm began. Back to when there was a nice man I met on the streets of Summerduck, a man I smiled with in the sunshine. A man who gave me back my ability to trust again after my ex and his friends convinced me all men were cheating, lying creeps.

And he was a bigger liar than the rest of them. He'd hidden the fact he was dead.

"I exist, Emma, and I love you."

His voice came from beside me. I looked over even as I splashed along the walkway through rivulets formed by the heavy downpour. His image was still there, transplanted like cellophane on my view of the buildings as I passed by.

"You don't exist. You're dead."

"I'm dead, but I'm still here. I can't leave until my brother vacates the old house. And now that I've met you, I don't want to leave."

Despite the rain, my steps slowed. "Say that again."

"I don't want to leave anymore. I want to stay here with you until it's your time to go."

"No. The part about your brother vacating the house."

"In life, Benjamin wanted the house more than anything, but it was mine. In a cosmic joke, he can never leave the house, and I can't enter."

"What happens if he leaves or you enter?"

"If I enter, I go into the afterlife and I never see you again. If he sets foot outside the building, he hopefully goes straight to hell."

"You don't like him."

His tone was a growl of disgust. "He stole from other people and from me. He drove away our sister's suitors. He destroyed a young woman's reputation. He killed people. And then he killed me. No, I don't like him."

"Why is he interfering with Bev modernizing the house? It won't affect him, will it?"

"No. But he thinks of the house as his. He likes the house the way it was while we were alive. He doesn't like to share, and he doesn't like other people being in charge and making decisions. He was always selfish."

"Could I try to bargain with him? Tell him if he'll let the electrical and plumbing work go through that he can pick out the fixtures and appliances?"

"You could try, but he knows you're my friend. He'll probably throw you out a window or something."

"Why did he attack Walter Clapp?"

"To scare everyone else off from invading his house.

Or, because he could. Or maybe, because he didn't like the smell of the fumigation chemicals."

"Ghosts can smell?"

"Barbeque drives me crazy."

"You love it?"

"I hate it. Do you know how frustrating it is to smell food when you can never eat again?"

I nodded dumbly and picked up my pace. The rain hadn't eased up and I finally noticed my shoes were getting soaked. I also realized I was beginning to believe him. "Would you be willing to talk to Bev outside the house? Tell her about your brother's presence inside?"

"You want me to frighten your friend when you don't really believe I'm here?"

"You're not here. I can see right through you."

"Not what I meant." He gave me the ghostly equivalent of an eyeroll.

"Bev needs to hear this from you. She won't believe me if I tell her about our conversations." We reached my house. "Coming in? If you do, you'll have to remain invisible entering or leaving. Aunt Jean would be upset if she saw a ghost, and there's no reason to upset her."

Something resembling humor laced his voice. "What does that say about Bev? You want me to upset her, just because I'm trapped as a spirit."

I unlocked the door and walked in, leaving my umbrella on the porch. When I looked around, I could see a faint image of Adam climbing the stairs to my second story apartment. Shutting the door and leaving my shoes on the landing, I followed him.

"What did you mean, trapped as a spirit?" I asked, heading to the bathroom for a towel to dry off.

When I didn't hear a reply, I returned to my living room to find Adam staring out a window. "Do you mind if I stay this way? It's hard work to appear solid, even when I'm dry."

"I'd rather you didn't appear solid while you're in here. I never know when one of my nosy neighbors will be checking up on my morals."

He began to pace the room. I was fascinated that the floorboards didn't creak even though logically I knew they shouldn't. I still had trouble wrapping my head around the fact he had no weight or bulk. "I tried to live a good life. I went to church. I tried not to lie or cheat. But dying, I cursed my twin brother. I prayed he'd never enjoy the house or the rewards of his thievery. I prayed he'd be tormented forever."

He stopped and looked at me. "Emma, we're not supposed to curse the ones who hurt us. I did, and instead of going to heaven, I'm stuck here. I've been made responsible for him, just as I was in life."

"Tell me how you know you're responsible for him? Is there some sort of afterlife cell phone network?"

"Don't mock what you don't understand."

"I'm not. I'm trying to comprehend how you know you're responsible for your brother, the same way I'm trying to figure out how to get your brother to allow the work to continue inside the house." I sat down, the towel wrapped around me for warmth. The temperature in my apartment had plummeted despite the soggy, sizzling air outside.

"I spent my life trying to keep my brother from hurting others. Benjamin loved to find a person's weakness and exploit it. Now I have to do the same thing in the afterlife."

"He certainly can hurt Bev by slowing down the work on the house."

"And he knows it. He must have heard her say how much she loves the house he loves. He has to win." His voice was grim.

"Will you talk to her? Will you tell her what you told me?" Again, I shamelessly begged.

"You don't think she'll run away screaming like you did?"

His words hit a nerve. "I didn't scream. And I was running to get out of the rain."

"Yeah." His tone was skeptical, but I'm sure I could make out a smile on his face.

"Will you talk to her? She won't hurt you."

"She can't hurt me. Living things can't hurt me now."

There was that aching sadness in his expression and in his voice again. I reached out a hand to him and felt only icy air.

"Remember? I don't have a body."

"But you did. And I'm sure it was a nice one."

"Are you flirting with me, Emma?" For an instant, he sounded as proudly masculine as Mike Randall.

"Yes." If you can't flirt with a ghost, who can you flirt with?

He gave a loud sigh. "All right. I'll talk to her, but away from the house. And only her. Prepare her first, and then think where you are. I'll come to you."

"Are you going to suddenly appear in front of us?"

A smile appeared on the see-through image of Adam. "Nothing like a little showmanship to convince someone you're a ghost."

A moment later, the image vanished.

"Adam? Adam?"

He was gone.

Chapter Eleven

It took me until the next morning after I'd arrived at work to summon up the nerve to call Bev. "I've learned something about your house. We need to meet, but at your current house, not the old Chadwick place."

"Ooh, you're being mysterious." She paused then and asked in a strained whisper, "This isn't good news, is it?"

"It might explain a lot of things. Is that good?"

"Maybe," she said. "Come over at lunch time, although I'll be watching the clock all morning. I'll call Roger and tell him to come home."

"No, don't. Not yet. Let me present this to you, and then we'll decide what to do from there."

"But it's his house, too."

"There's someone else involved, and it's his story, not mine. Roger won't mind missing this meeting. You may decide this is nothing but a waste of time, and Roger wouldn't appreciate us wasting his time during office hours."

"Actually, today is surgery day."

"Even better not to involve him yet. I'll see you at noon."

Bev wasn't the only one watching the clock. What if Adam didn't show up? Maybe I was crazy. Maybe he got waterlogged walking to my apartment in the storm and couldn't look like a person any more. Maybe he got recalled to heaven or got his angel wings. To him, that would be more important than human worries.

I tried to bury myself in my work, but all I managed to do was keep from making too many mistakes. My mind was on Bev and how she'd take my news.

Finally, after what felt like centuries, it was noon. I hurried out of the shop and walked over to Bev's in record time. She met me at the front door and led me to the kitchen where she had muffins, fruit, and coffee ready. I poured a cup of coffee and grabbed a muffin, taking a big bite while I kept thinking, *Adam, I'm here. Please show up.*

"Hey, wait for your guest," Bev said.

"I don't think he'll mind."

"Really, Em, where are your manners?"

"She's right, I don't mind," came from a familiar baritone behind her.

Bev turned around, saw Adam, and jumped back a half-step. "Oh, my goodness. I didn't hear you come in."

"You wouldn't. I'm a ghost."

Bev gave me a dirty look. "I'm not in the mood for parlor games."

I shook my head. "He's not kidding."

"Touch me," Adam said.

I was a little jealous. He'd never given me an offer like

that.

Bev put out her hand. Her fingers went through him before she jumped back a full step and held her hand with the other one. "You're so cold."

"And not solid."

She stared at him. "You look solid."

"I've found it's easier to talk to people if you show yourself. I could talk to you without appearing, and you'd accuse Emma of using a radio or something."

"Who are you?"

"In life I was Adam Chadwick, the one who was killed in the barn outside your new house. My twin brother Benjamin resides inside your house and is causing your troubles."

Bev turned and faced me, looking like she'd burst into tears at any moment. "This isn't funny."

"I know. Adam says Benjamin always wanted the house and now he can't leave it. Or he could leave it, but then he would go to his reward."

"I can't go in to ask him, but I think he's having too much fun ruining your plans for his house to leave voluntarily," Adam told her.

Bev faced Adam, taking a step away from him. Her face had lost most of its color, and her voice was shaky. "But we bought the house. It isn't in your family anymore."

"We're dead. We don't care about ownership."

She pulled out a chair and collapsed into it. "What am I going to do?"

Adam paced a couple of steps across the kitchen and

back. "I don't know. I didn't know what to do about Benjamin in life. As a spirit, he can do anything."

"What about an exorcism?" I asked. "He's an evil spirit who needs help getting to the afterlife."

"Who does exorcisms?" Bev asked.

"The Catholic church."

"But we're not Catholic."

"Well, ask them. Or Google exorcisms. I don't know." I was as uncomfortable as she was with evil spirits. The only one I'd seen before this was in a movie, and I don't think that girl's head could really spin around without special effects.

Bev turned back to Adam. "Do you have any ideas?"

He shrugged. "I know Benjamin's in your house, just like I know I can't go inside. I know he's as difficult to get along with as he was in life, but that could just be my opinion. We never got along."

"Can you talk to him through a window?"

"Of course, Bev. May I call you Bev?" he asked with gentlemanly manners.

Nothing charms a woman like a man with good manners. Bev was no exception. She smiled at him. "Yes. I wondered if you could ask him what it would take for him to allow us to make our changes. Except for repairing the roof, we'd leave the attic untouched for him. Sort of his own space."

"I'll ask him if you'd like."

"Could you do it now, please? And then if it doesn't work, I'll find someone who does exorcisms."

I grabbed another muffin and a handful of grapes and followed them out of the house and up the street, munching away with the knowledge that this would be all I'd get for lunch.

We walked into the front yard. Adam looked around to make sure no one was around and then leaped up to the second story window. To anyone else, he appeared to be standing on the porch roof. I knew better.

He tapped on the window. "Ben. Open up."

I don't know what I expected. I saw the window open, clearly showing the face that I'd seen in the glass. "What do you want?" It was the first time I'd heard the ghost speak. He had a gravelly, angry, belligerent voice.

I stepped farther into the yard, Bev following me. We looked up at the window and for the first time got a clear view of Benjamin Chadwick. He had dark hair, a mustache, a hatchet for a nose, and a cruel mouth. What grabbed my attention were his eyes. They were dark, impenetrable, icy.

"The lady down there bought the house. She wants to make changes. Modernize the appliances, the plumbing, paint, fix the roof. She says she won't touch the attic, except for repairs. In exchange, she wants you to leave the workmen alone."

"Why?"

"Why not?"

"This is my house. Now and forever. Go away." Benjamin slammed the window, cracking the glass pane.

Adam glanced around, then floated to the ground with ease. He walked over to us and said, "You heard?"

"Yes. He wanted us to, didn't he?" I asked.

He nodded.

"Then I guess I'd better find an exorcist. You need to tell me everything you can about your brother," Bev said. She glared up at the window. If I were Benjamin, I'd look out. Bev could be both persuasive and stubborn.

At that moment, we heard shouting from inside. We hurried around to the back where the workmen were. Mr. Ellery, the chief electrician, came out of the house a moment after we started asking the painters what happened.

He bore down on Bev. "We can't work on your electrical wires. No one can. Everything was going fine, we followed all safety procedures, and all of a sudden, we're getting shocked. We put meters on the outlets and got abnormally high voltage."

"Anyone hurt?" she asked.

"Not seriously. But there's no explanation. It's impossible. And we can't work with this danger."

"There must be a second electrical feed into the house. It's an old house. Didn't they do things like that back then?" Bev asked, grasping for any possibility but the one on both our minds.

"We've followed every wire. The only place juice is coming into the house is through the box. We locked it out, and we were still getting shocked."

Blast. It had to be Benjamin Chadwick's ghost summoning up supernatural energy. I shocked myself by how easily I could believe this possible. But then, we weren't having a normal year in Summerduck. At least, I wasn't.

"You mustn't have done it right." Bev went on the offensive.

"Don't tell me my job, lady. We did it right. Your house has some sort of weird, other-worldly source of power, and it keeps shocking us."

"But—"

"I'll send you my bill."

Ellery's assistant had finished packing up. The two men shouldered their tools and walked around to the front of the house. We followed them and stood watching as they climbed into the van and drove off.

The three of us started our walk back to Bev's current residence, spirits drooping.

Adam said, "I was the firstborn twin. Benjamin was born a few minutes later. Because of that, our father considered me his first born and his heir in everything.

"Maybe that was what turned Ben into a horror, but even as a child, he was cruel. He'd beat up other children, lie, steal, cause trouble. We didn't look alike, so he couldn't blame much on me. Everyone knew to watch out for Benjamin."

I was fascinated. "What did your parents think?"

"My father was stern. Wrath-of-God stern. He was always whipping Ben. Then Ben would run to Mama and she'd make everything better. Feed him pie while I was sent out to take care of the chickens and carry in firewood. I mean, he'd be punished because he did something wrong, but I'd have to do his chores and mine.

When she wasn't looking, Ben would make faces at me. He knew he was 'playing her'. I think that's your modern expression."

He sounded resigned. I didn't know you could feel sorry for a ghost, but I did. I was finding myself having all sorts of odd feelings for Adam. The weirdest ones I put down to having a crush on him. He was so unlike the eligible men I met daily that I decided having a crush on him was inevitable. Any woman would. He was kind, polite, funny, and he had a sort of wounded sorrow that made him sympathetic.

But there was no way I could fall in love with a ghost. Could I?

"Where did you learn our modern expressions?" Bev asked, suddenly suspicious. She unlocked her door and let us in. Perhaps because she knew Adam could enter anyway, and there was no reason for the two of us to stand on her porch. It was hot out.

"I've been wandering around town ever since I died. I listen to people, even if I can no longer join in their conversations." He smiled then. "Well, not without scaring them."

That set off alarm bells for me. I swallowed a grape and asked, "You were wandering around outside your house for days before Benjamin died? Why didn't you go straight to Heaven?"

"Because you can't get into Heaven with a load of hate in your heart. And I was consumed by my hatred for my brother after he killed me, and long after he died. By the sixties or seventies, I had forgiven him, but by then, Benjamin was well established in the house and up to his old tricks. He was harming the living who entered the house. I decided to stay and try to help others avoid my fate."

"It's as easy as that. You decided to stay?" This was different than the theology I heard in church.

"I asked to stay and try to make amends for the sins of my brother against the living until he leaves for wherever he's bound. My request was granted." There was that smile that I was falling in love with again. "The Ultimate Decision-Maker feels that my soul has some growing left to do."

Bev's jaw dropped. She managed to shut it enough to ask, "You talk to God?"

"Don't you?"

"But do you actually hear his voice?"

"Loud and clear. Perhaps because my body no longer gets in the way."

There was awe in my voice now. "What does he say?"

"That I still don't get it. He has a plan for me other than attempting to block my brother's crueler designs. He's angry with me because I've not yet learned to be obedient to His will."

"Ghosts can disobey God?" Wow. I never expected to have this conversation.

"That's why we're ghosts. We can't enter Heaven with a load of hate and worldly problems in our hearts. We haven't learned to let go and obey. And in my case, He has a plan for me that I've not yet seen."

"When will this happen?" How much longer would Adam be earthbound? I couldn't decide if I wanted him in Heaven more, or if I wanted him here with me.

And that let me know I was falling in love with Adam Chadwick, nice guy and ghost.

"In God's time." He gave me a radiant smile. "I've learned He has his own timetable. He'll let me know when."

Talk of obeying and time made me look at the clock. Taking a handful of grapes with me, I headed for the door to return to work. "I've overstayed my lunch hour. Bev, good luck finding an exorcist. Adam, good luck on—," what do you wish for a ghost you've developed a friendship with? "—your timetable."

* * *

As we waited on the local parish priest a few days later, Bev admitted to me that she gave the man an edited version of events. Accidents were mentioned. Odd occurrences were mentioned. Talking to ghosts was not. "He's going to bless the house in case there is some malevolent element causing these incidents. He did say no one knows exactly what kind of evil residue is left in old houses after over a century of people living in them."

Father Smith was a gray-haired man who wore a clerical collar with a black suit. He had a commanding presence and a hurried air as he approached Bev and me with a greeting and a firm handshake. He called on the workmen, painters that day, to join us inside while the house was blessed. I heard one of the men say, "About time with this joker of a house," as we all filed onto the front porch.

Bev turned the handle of the front door and the priest sprinkled holy water over the doorway. He said a brief prayer in his booming voice and received a ragged chorus of amens. In each room on the main floor, he went through the same process, calling on the Lord, Jesus, and St. Joseph as he prayed and sprinkled holy water from a small flask.

We ended at the front door again. A couple of the workmen thanked Father Smith and said, "See you on Sunday." Bev and I both thanked him, Bev gave him a donation to the church, and he drove away in his small, faded blue car with a dent in the back fender.

"Well, let's hope that released our evil ghost," Bev said as she locked the front door and we left.

An hour later, I got a call at work. At first all I heard was sobbing. I looked at the number. "Bev. What's wrong?"

"That ghost tried to kill us," she wailed.

"Us?"

"I took the roofer up to the attic. I thought it would be safe now. He pointed out what I already knew and wrote some notes. On the third step down, someone or something had removed a board. I fell trying to keep from falling in the hole."

"Are you all right?"

"Yes. Just some bruises. I caught myself on the railing. But Emma, the step was there when we went up." She burst into tears again.

The ghostly terror was upping his game and he didn't care how often or how many living people he hurt. "Well, blessing the house didn't help," I said more to myself than her.

"That's not very helpful," she snapped. At least it seemed to stop the tears. "Benjamin Chadwick is still there. What am I going to do?"

"You need someone to give the house an exorcism from top to bottom. Maybe that'll catch your ghost."

"I did hear about one preacher who does exorcisms. He's from one of the snake charming sects."

"I'd say it's time to call in the big guns. Have you told Roger?"

"He wouldn't believe any of this."

Worse, I would have said he wouldn't notice any of this. "Are you going to tell him?"

"No. I'm going to hire the exorcist. If he's successful, I won't have to tell Roger."

"And if he's not?"

"Don't say that, Em. We have to be positive. I love that house."

I closed my eyes and shook my head. So did the ghost.

Chapter Twelve

Mike Randall stopped by the shop at quitting time wearing civvies. Dress civvies for him, which consisted of pressed khaki slacks and a dark polo shirt. When he walked into the crowded art supply sales floor, my first thought came out of my mouth before I thought how it sounded. "Are you here to see me or are you still looking for Adam Chadwick?"

"Both. Let's see if we can find him, and then I'll take you out to dinner."

"If we find him, you'll spend hours taking him to the station and booking him for assault. Sounds like a handy way not to take a girl out to dinner."

"I'm off duty. I just want to talk to him. Find out where he lives so we can talk to him again, officially, if necessary. You'll get fed."

I knew my skepticism was in my tone and on my face. "At what hour?"

"Have some faith, Sugarbear."

"Oh, all right." I'd already seen evidence at Bev's that I could send messages to Adam by my thoughts. As I said goodnight to Mrs. Nelson, the owner, and picked up my purse, I was silently telling Adam to vanish for a while.

We drove up and down the streets in the old neighborhood for fifteen minutes before Mike said, "No luck tonight. Let's get something to eat. Chinese okay?"

It wasn't the Cannon, but the small Chinese/Japanese/Thai restaurant on the road past the big box stores had the best Asian food in town. We went in and were directed to a table where Mike sat facing the door as always.

After we ordered beef with broccoli and chicken with mixed vegetables to share, and I poured both of us tiny cups of steaming green tea, Mike asked, "How's Bev's house coming?"

"Slowly. They're still plagued by accidents."

"Even though she had one of the priests at St. Matthew's bless the house?"

I looked Mike square in the eye. "You heard about that?"

He gave me a complacent smile. "There's not much we don't hear about."

"I think someone or something doesn't want her to renovate the house."

"Like your ghost that tied up Walter Clapp?"

"It's not *my* ghost." Our soup came and we stopped talking to eat the fragrant broth. "Bev called me this afternoon to say while she and the roofer were in the attic, someone removed one of the steps. No one else was in the house. Removing the step made no noise. It was a step near the top and neither she nor the roofer heard or saw anything."

He stared at me for a full minute. I could almost hear the hamsters in his head running around on their wheels. "Sounds like someone has it out for Ms. Myers. Someone who can move quietly and knows how to make it look like an accident."

"This doesn't look like an accident. They'd gone up those steps just a few minutes before, and the step wasn't missing. It wasn't even loose."

"Does she want to file a report?"

"No, Mike. Bev's reached the same conclusion as me. There's an evil spirit in that house."

He shook his head. "We don't arrest evil spirits. We arrest bad guys. And a hundred times out of a hundred, bad stuff is done by bad guys."

Our dinner arrived, stopping me from challenging his opinion. About the time I'd eaten half my dinner and two bites of Mike's, I resumed the discussion. "Nobody's that quiet. And nobody has it in for Bev."

"Has she ever met this Adam Chadwick guy?"

"Yes. She met him for the first time a few days ago."

"You're sure?"

"Yes, Mike. I introduced them. He has nothing against her."

"She has his house."

Whoa. What had Randall learned about the Chadwicks? "She bought the house from the estate of a dead man. Mr. Duffy."

"What if this Chadwick thinks he has a claim on this house? Would he go after the current owners?"

"Adam's a happy-go-lucky type with little interest in material things. He wouldn't want the house. It would only tie him down." That was the truth. Sort of. Well, it was the only truth I thought Randall would buy.

"A modern-day hippy." There was a scoffing note in his voice.

"I suppose." Anything to keep Mike from looking too closely at Adam.

"Who else would have an interest in stopping the Myers from renovating the house and moving in?"

"Else?"

"Besides Adam."

"Forget Adam. How about Mrs. Carmichael? She's being very difficult about the renovation. First it was tearing down the barn. Then the paint color. I don't know what she'd have against Bev, though."

He smiled. "I'll keep her in mind."

I smiled back. "Because you don't like her, either."

He turned serious in an instant. "We don't act on the basis of whether we like someone, but on the facts. You know that's the only way for the legal system to operate."

"The fact that she's a royal pain has nothing to do with why she makes the best suspect in this instance?"

Mike gave me a wink, but he didn't say a word, in a rare show of diplomacy.

"Personally, I believe it's an evil ghost, but since you don't like that explanation, you might want to consider her."

"Can you imagine Mrs. Carmichael sneaking up two

flights of stairs and removing a stair tread without anyone hearing or noticing her?" Mike was grinning now, his seriousness dissolved in the laughter he was holding back.

"No." That was the problem. I knew the culprit was a ghost named Benjamin Chadwick. I just couldn't prove it to Sergeant Mike Randall without putting my relationship with Adam in danger.

"Did anyone else want to buy the house when the Myers bought it?"

"Not that I've heard of." Another possibility that really wasn't one.

"Well, if you end up with an exorcism, call me, will you? I'd like to see that." Now he was laughing.

* * *

When I called Bev the next day to tell her about our dinner date and Mike's suggestion someone was deliberately sabotaging the restoration efforts, she interrupted me. "Things have gotten worse, and Roger has run out of patience with the house. Meet me over there, will you?"

I walked in the once-elegant front doorway to hear Roger say, "This is the last straw. We can't live here, and we can't fix the place up. We'll have to sell, and at a substantial loss, too."

I was about to quietly back out of the house when a teary-eyed Bev appeared from the direction of the kitchen and spotted me. "The roofers quit. Their safety line broke in two."

She held up two pieces of heavy line that appeared to

have been ripped apart. Not cut, but ripped by some incredible force and singed at the tips.

"How did that happen?"

"The man began walking around on the roof and all of a sudden, bang. He turned around to see the lines sizzling and fraying like you see it now. There was no one else around. He managed to hang on until his coworkers rescued him. I was in the kitchen and heard the shouting. They said we're haunted."

I remembered the face in the upstairs window in my photos. "He saw a ghost break the line?"

"The house isn't haunted," Roger said.

"Then how do you explain all the strange things that have happened to the workmen here?" I asked. Bev gave a minute shake of her head in reply.

Roger shot me a look. "Carelessness. Getting in over their heads because the job was too big and needing an excuse to bail on us. Faulty equipment. Faulty wiring in an old house. There are any number of perfectly rational explanations. I have to get back to the hospital. I'll let you decide what the next step is, but I don't want to throw any more money on renovating this house if the job can't be done." Roger kissed the top of Bev's head and walked out.

I stood there, not certain if I should stay or go.

Bev remained rooted to the spot, her arms wrapped around her middle. "When I told him I saw a ghost," she said in a quiet voice, "he laughed at me."

I knew Bev could be dangerous when she spoke

quietly and calmly. "He doesn't believe in what he doesn't see." I knew a lot of people like that.

She glared at me. "He wasn't concerned if I'd lost my mind or if there are really ghosts roaming our town. He found my story ludicrous. He just laughed. How dare he?"

"Maybe he found it easier to ignore what he doesn't believe than to deal with it. You're his rock. If anything happens to you, his world falls apart."

She gave me a scoffing look and rolled her eyes.

"Bev, how do you think Roger faces the blood and gore of the operating room, patients dying, the constant workload? Because you hold the world together for him. Maybe he can't handle any sign of illness or weakness in you because his whole world would unravel?"

"I didn't tell him I was dying. I told him I saw a ghost."

"He could handle a medical diagnosis better. He understands that. You just threw something at him that he can't comprehend."

She studied me through narrowed eyes. "You sure?"

"Yeah. You'd have gotten the same reaction if you'd told him Martians had moved into the attic."

"At least he could see Martians."

* * *

When I answered the phone the next day at work, I was greeted with "Em, I hope this time I've found the solution."

I knew Bev wouldn't give up. "What?"

"One of the painters belongs to an ultra-conservative sect that believes in evil spirits and the power of the devil. He told his preacher, the Reverend Durrell, about our house blessing, and the man called to find out if the troubles we've been having went away."

"What did you tell him?"

"I told him no. Not after that step was removed while we were in the attic."

"Bev, are you sure the painter didn't remove it so you'd hire his preacher?"

"Emma, I was in the attic bored to tears. It was roasting up there. I kept looking down the stairwell, hoping we'd be done soon so I could get someplace cooler and do something more interesting. No one, no living person, could have removed that step without my seeing and hearing them."

"When is this preacher coming to the house?"

"Saturday morning."

I saw an immediate problem. "What about Roger?"

"He's covering that day for someone in the practice."

"Can I bring Mike Randall? When I first told him I thought a ghost attacked Walter Clapp and we might do an exorcism, he said he wanted to watch." I didn't tell her he found the whole idea entertaining. She had enough ridicule from her husband.

"So, you and Sergeant Randall are getting friendly."

I wanted to wipe the smirk out of her voice. "No. I'm just trying to keep him from putting out a BOLO on Adam."

"He is a good-looking man."

"Adam?"

"No. Mike. A good-looking, living man."

I sighed. There was no hope for this conversation as long as Bev was trying to find Mr. Right for me. Although why she'd pick Randall, who was very open about only wanting to bed me, went beyond reason. I grumbled, "What time Saturday?"

"Nine."

"He wants to kick out the evil spirit before it gets well caffeinated?"

"No, he wants to drive the ghost away with your terrible jokes."

"Or the preacher could have Mike Randall spout some of his obnoxious opinions about everyone and everything that isn't Mike Randall. No, wait. That would drive out everyone but the ghost. Benjamin Chadwick in life was apparently as self-centered and bigoted as Mike." Fortunately, we were talking on the phone so Bev couldn't see the steam rising from my scalp.

"Don't be so touchy. And of course you can invite Sergeant Randall." Bev sounded like she was gloating.

I'd have to make sure Adam stayed far away from the Chadwick house on Saturday morning.

Chapter Thirteen

Unlike Father Smith from St. Matthew's, preacher Durrell drove up in a new Cadillac sedan. I reminded myself they might both replace their cars every ten years but be on different cycles. That didn't stop the words "snake oil salesman" from echoing in my head.

A snake oil salesman who didn't shy away from down home Southern cooking. He looked like he never met a biscuit he didn't like, particularly with gravy.

Like the priest, the Reverend Mr. Durrell was middle-aged and had commanding mannerisms and a booming voice. Unlike the priest, who seemed slightly embarrassed to be praying over a house rather than people, the preacher appeared to view this as an everyday occurrence. "Don't you fret, Ms. Myers. The devil tries to sneak in any way he can. Our job is to fight him off. We need to pray."

And pray we did in the front yard. When we finished and I thought it was safe to open my eyes, Mike Randall was standing next to me in uniform. Mike leaned over and gestured toward the young patrol officer who stood just behind him. "Jim's a member of Reverend Durrell's flock."

I nodded to patrol officer Jim and he gave me one sharp jerk of his head in return. I wondered if this was his first day on the job. He looked young enough to still be in high school, in a Wally Cleaver and Mouseketeer sort of way.

We were joined by one of the painters I'd seen here and two older men, who greeted the minister and nodded to Bev and me. They were probably members of the Reverend's church. I wondered if they'd seen an exorcism before. The bad feeling in the pit of my stomach made me wish I wasn't here.

Bev led the way up the steps and onto the porch. Before she could unlock the door, the preacher held up his hands and shut his eyes. "In the name of Jesus Christ, I command all evil spirits to leave this house."

It felt staged. I'd seen too many lawyers perform in court. Right then, I knew he was performing. This wouldn't accomplish anything but relieve Bev of her money.

The painter and the other two men shouted "Hallelujah." Their belief and honesty rolled off them. I was glad they were coming into the house with us.

The preacher then nodded to Bev and she unlocked the door. We all trooped into the living room, where Reverend Durrell led us in prayer again. Then he turned to Bev. "Where does the devil seem to be strongest?"

"Upstairs, the second room facing the front of the house," I replied. The room where I'd first seen the face in the window. The room where I couldn't breathe the first day I set foot in this house.

"Then let us go there and confront the devil in his lair," the preacher said, gesturing for me to lead the way.

I didn't want to. I already knew the ghost didn't like me. He'd tried to choke me in that room the day I'd met Adam.

Noting my feet were dragging, the preacher said, "Lead on fearlessly. You have the Christ with you."

Personally, I believed I had the Holy Trinity with me. I also had an actor playing a preacher at my back. Sending up a prayer to obey God's will, I started up the stairs.

I knew I had a slew of witnesses if Benjamin Chadwick made an appearance. That might make a believer out of Roger. The group straggled up the stairs behind me and collected in the hallway. I pointed to the open doorway.

The preacher began to pray as he walked forward, the men of his congregation following closely and offering up amens and hallelujahs. Bev and I trailed behind, Mike Randall in the rear. I glanced back at Mike. He was looking all around, assessing the possibilities for mayhem.

Once I entered the room, I felt someone pass behind me. I didn't pay any attention to who had walked by, thinking it was Mike.

A booming laugh rang out in the room. I looked around me and saw everyone else doing the same. None of us had made that sound.

"The evil one is here," the preacher proclaimed. "In the name of Jesus Christ, I demand that you leave this house."

"This is my house," a man's voice said. "You're trespassing. Go away."

"Benjamin?" I asked. My voice squeaked.

"If it isn't my brother's tart. Trying to get the house back for him, are you?" The voice sounded as if it relished the opportunity to tell us off.

"Adam doesn't want the house, but you can't have it. It's left your family, and now you must leave."

"Never."

The preacher began again in a shaky voice, demanding the evil spirit in the room depart this house.

"You're supposed to pass over into the next world," I said to the ceiling. I wouldn't suggest Heaven. I didn't want to put God in a bind. "Leave now."

"Never." I felt a cold vein wrap around me in the warm house. Then I could no longer breathe. My lungs ached as I tried to pull oxygen in, but there was no air. I felt like I was underwater. Spots swam before my eyes. I slumped to the floor, gasping as the preacher continued to pray, his congregants responding enthusiastically.

Mike knelt down next to me checking my pulse. I was too weak to care if he started CPR on me. Too weak to be frightened that I didn't care if he put his hands all over me.

Through the thudding in my ears, I heard the preacher ask God to strengthen us for the coming battle against the powers of evil. He went on and on, his voice gaining strength as he continued. He sounded like he was leading a revival meeting.

The cold was off me now, letting me breathe. The heat that filled the air around me left me soggy with sweat. I started to sit up with Mike's help and Bev's hovering while the preacher and his followers prayed for the forces of evil to leave the house.

The voice roared, "I will not go!"

"God wants you to go to your reward," I said and stood up.

"You're thinking my punishment."

I walked over to the other window in the room. The one where I'd never seen his face appear. I yanked and pulled until I had it wide open. "Go on. God is calling you."

"I don't care to listen." As I looked on in shock, I saw one man after another levitated and thrown screaming from the room until only Mike and the preacher were left. Reverend Durrell kept praying until he was picked up by an unseen force. Then he began to cry and pray in a begging voice as he was carried to the top of the stairs. He screamed as he shot forward into space.

There was a loud thud, and then the house was silent.

Mike rushed out of the room, leaping over the fallen and ran down the stairs. I followed, and by the time I reached the banister and looked down, he was checking out the preacher. "Call an ambulance," he shouted.

I grabbed my phone from my pocket and dialed 911. I told the dispatcher the address and that we had a man who had fallen down a flight of stairs and was unconscious. Then, ignoring Bev, who was sobbing behind me, I took the phone down to Mike.

He barely noticed me as he took my phone. He started talking to the dispatcher, sounding every inch a police officer, as he continued checking the preacher for broken bones and bleeding.

I went back up the stairs and began to check on the parishioners who'd been tossed into the hallway.

"Where's that devil?" one of the older men said. "We need to drive him back to hell."

"Let's get medical help for the preacher first. Are you all right?" I asked.

"Yes," the man said to me. "George, you okay?" he asked the other parishioner.

George was having a cut on his head seen to by the rookie cop, whose hands shook. "Fine. Stop fussing, Jim. You need to see to your friend, little lady. Jason, you all right?"

The painter shook himself off like a wet dog. "Yeah, I'm okay."

I looked around for Bev and found her sitting on the floor just inside the bedroom, sobbing loudly. I walked through the doorway and was slammed in the jaw. Dropping on my butt, I scooted over to Bev and took her hand. "Let's get out of here."

"He won't let me."

"Inch toward me."

Bev started to slide on her butt as I backed up, still holding hands. The sound of sirens told me the ambulance would be here in a minute. "Is that for the preacher?" she asked.

"Yes. I didn't realize Mike handled medical

emergencies so well." I kept backing up, my bottom sweeping the floor, as I pulled Bev along with me. I kept talking, either to distract Bev, Benjamin Chadwick, or me. I wasn't sure who needed to be distracted the most.

I made it to the hallway. The young patrol officer, Jim, grabbed Bev's wrist and the two of us jerked her out of the room. The door slammed closed behind us.

Bev shrieked and squeezed my hand.

The ghost was either very possessive of that room or of his privacy.

Jim helped Bev to her feet while I jumped up and looked over the balcony. Mike was still focused on the Reverend Durrell, who was now moaning.

Glancing back at Bev, I said, "He's alive."

"Thank God for that." She spoke to the other men, who'd risen shakily, and then started down the steps to Mike and the preacher as the paramedics came in with their stretcher.

I looked at the young policeman. "You and Mike are going to have some interesting paperwork to fill out. Unexplained levitations. A disembodied voice ordering you out of the house. I don't envy the two of you turning that in."

"I don't have to explain it, ma'am. I just have to report it correctly."

He sounded so young and so stern I almost smiled. "Good. Before this, Mike didn't believe in ghosts. I wonder what he'll say now."

"Probably quite a bit." Jim nodded to me and headed

downstairs.

The paramedics told the man with the head wound to go to the emergency room or see his doctor and took the preacher, one of his legs splinted, out on a stretcher.

Mike handed me back my cell phone. "I'll need to report this. I'm sure it'll get kicked around City Hall, but I doubt they'll do anything."

His solemn tone and expression made me ask, "Still don't believe in ghosts?"

"There was something evil there that I couldn't see. Something otherworldly. Were you hurt?"

"He didn't pick Bev or me up. Or you or Jim. I guess he doesn't attack women or men in uniform. He did smash me in the face when I went back in to get Bev, and she said he wouldn't let her out of the room."

He looked around. "She's out now."

"I know. Jim helped me get her out. His instincts are good. How's Reverend Durrell?"

"Broken leg. Probable concussion. I'm not sure about other injuries." His abrupt answers told me he was still in police operation mode. In a way, that was comforting.

"I'm glad you were here today."

"I wasn't expecting what happened."

"No one was." I began to tremble.

"I wonder why Reverend Durrell couldn't drive out the evil spirit? Jim said he's done it before successfully."

I stared in the direction of the second-floor bedroom, picturing it as it appeared with all of us there. "Maybe he doesn't see himself as an evil spirit. Maybe he sees himself as a ghost who's been wronged. Maybe he sees the men trying to change his environment as the bad guys."

"In which case, he'd see you and Bev as the chief baddies. Yet he didn't throw the two of you out. Makes you wonder what he has planned for you. Stay out of this house, Em. You and Bev. That's an order."

"An order?" Bev exclaimed. That was like waving a red flag in front of a bull.

"What's going to happen to the house?" I asked before a livid Bev could scream at Mike.

"I suspect the city will condemn the house until they figure out what is going on."

"So, just like that, the ghost wins." Bev's hands were in fists.

"Yeah." Mike looked over my shoulder and added, "Sorry, Bev. You can't have whatever it is throwing people down stairs. The house is bound to be quarantined or condemned."

"All the money we've spent on it. Our dreams. The mortgage." With every word, Bev turned paler.

"Don't faint on me," I said, putting my arms around her.

"I'm not going to faint. I might scream or pull out my hair, but I'm not going to faint. How am I going to hide this from Roger? He has enough to worry about without having to deal with renovating a condemned house." The look she gave Mike should have knocked him to the ground.

Ignoring her, Mike gestured to the other men. "Let's

go." As they filed out, he turned to us. "Out of the house. Both of you. Now."

Chapter Fourteen

I might have put up an argument, but Bev walked out of the house, her beloved and now off-limits house, shoulders drooping. I glared at Randall as I followed. We stood on the sidewalk and watched him drive off in his patrol car with Jim the rookie.

"Roger is going to be furious," Bev kept repeating as we walked over to her house. The storm clouds building in the southwestern sky seemed to be nature's warning of a blow-up in the Myers house that night.

Bev second-guessed every decision she'd made about the house. She regretted wanting to buy the majestic Victorian structure. She was sorry she talked Roger into putting in an offer. Over and over, she went on berating herself.

When we entered her house, the phone rang. From the half of the conversation I could make out, Roger had seen the x-rays of Reverend Durrell's broken leg and had heard the entire story of the haunted house. A tale that was spreading around the hospital like wildfire. What was this about them owning a haunted house?

From the volume of his indecipherable words, he was

furious. Bev was in tears, apologizing for everything.

I slipped out the front door, knowing she'd call me when she wanted someone to listen. My feet and the strong gusts of wind warning of the approaching storm carried me back to the Chadwick house.

"Adam, we need to talk. Now."

I thought he'd appear beside me as I walked along, but I didn't see him. I stood in front of the house for a few moments, gathering my courage.

Then I headed around the house past shingles stacked on the ground before I chickened out.

I knew the back door was unlocked. I walked in past paint cans and painting tarps in the back hall. "Hello?" My voice quavered. "Benjamin? Make an appearance. I want to talk to you."

No answer. The house was gloomy with the storm clouds blocking the sun. I wasn't about to turn on the few ceiling lights, expecting Benjamin to drop one on my head.

I climbed the stairs in the gloom, watching all around me and trembling. This wouldn't work if I didn't appear confident. I swallowed and then called out, "Benjamin. Show yourself. It's not like you to hide."

I stood in the doorway to the big bedroom Benjamin Chadwick had staked out as his. "Come on, Ben. No games. Let's talk."

Benjamin Chadwick appeared before me in solid form. As often as Adam had pulled that trick, it still frightened me. Especially since Benjamin materialized looking furious. His expression said he planned to kill me.

Thunder sounded again, closer this time.

Then he stepped back and bowed me into the room. "You want to bargain with me."

"Yes. Your interests and Bev's are not mutually exclusive. You live on different planes. Let them renovate the house and live here, unmolested, while you continue to reside here without making an appearance or harming anyone."

"Why?"

"Why not?"

"There's no fun in good behavior. Look at Adam. No fun. No daring. So boring. I couldn't stand the obedient little fair- haired boy when we were both in the cradle."

He strolled toward the open window. "Now, you, on the other hand, are interesting. I bet you break the rules with flair."

I thought I'd try to build a rapport with the evil spirit. "I'm breaking one just coming in here to talk to you."

"Good. It gets lonely not having anyone to talk to."

"Then don't you want to go to the afterlife? You'd have people just like yourself to talk to."

I didn't know ghosts could snort, but Benjamin snorted at my question. "You think hell is inviting? I don't think so. And I know where my beliefs will send me the second I leave this structure."

"Then the best solution would be to behave yourself and allow Bev and Roger to remodel the house and live in it while you reside alongside of them, listening in to their conversations."

"In silence? Behaving myself? Please. That would be its own form of hell. And what is Adam's suggestion?"

"Burning down the house."

"No!" I'd never seen a rage so sudden or intense. He leaped at me and I felt ice surround my throat and traveled downward inside my body. I couldn't breathe. Stabbing pain gripped my lungs. Pounding echoed in my head. I tried to pull away, but I carried the pain and the ice with me.

"Ben!" called a voice from behind me.

I fell to the floor with a jolt as Benjamin moved to the open window. "Get in here or I kill her."

"Kill her and I'll burn down the house."

Some sort of supernatural fireworks went off at the window. I didn't stick around to watch. I ran out of the room and down the stairs.

I raced out the back door, knowing Benjamin couldn't leave the confines of the house, and collided with Adam's freezing hologram on the porch. He took a step back and studied my face. "Did he hurt you?"

All I could do was stare at Adam.

"Did he hurt you?"

I shook my head no and burst into sobs. "You can't go in there. You shouldn't even be on the porch."

Already he seemed to have faded, and if it began to rain he'd become translucent. "He tried to kill you, didn't he?" His tone was hard.

"Let's get off the porch. Go somewhere and talk about this." Thunder rumbled nearby.

Adam shook his head. "Look at those bruises. He did

try to kill you."

It hurt to talk. My chest felt like someone had punched me repeatedly. "Yes, but it could have been worse."

"It stops now." He sounded grim. Determined.

And I was determined he wouldn't get hurt by his brother. "You can't stop it. I tried. He doesn't want to stop. And you can't go in there."

"I'm the only one who can stop it. As long as a Chadwick lived there, I didn't want to act. But he's tried to kill you, your friends, the workmen. He has to be stopped."

"Let someone else stop him." I wrapped my arms around my waist. Wished they were Adam's arms and knew they never could be. "Adam, he's your brother."

"And my murderer. If he hadn't been stabbed by the rusty pitchfork in the barn, he'd have lived a long life enjoying what was mine by right as the firstborn." He picked up some rags the painters had been using, now lying in a corner of the porch. The smell immediately made me jerk back. Before I could stop him, he flung the rags through the open doorway.

He unscrewed the top of a can of turpentine and tossed it inside. Then he glared into the house until fire flickered and then grew. He stood before me as the flames licked up the far wall and across the floor. He moved around me, into me, surrounding me, and I felt cold but safe. He possessed me, pouring love and kindness into me. When he finally stepped away, I was breathless.

The rags were crisp, the walls glowed, and the ceiling smoldered. "Adam."

"He can't leave the house. If the house is gone, his soul goes to where it belongs."

Lightning lit the sky and thunder boomed. It would pour down rain any second. "The rain will put out the fire."

"If God is merciful, the house will burn to the foundations." He stared into my eyes. "Emma, I will always love you."

The fire was spreading and heat and smoke now poured out the back door. Through the fire, I could see the ceiling glowed. Then the old, unpainted walls burst into a ball of fire.

A man's voice called from inside, "Join me, Adam."

"Never. It's time you faced things alone, Ben," Adam called into the doorway. His time on the porch had made him fade like old cloth in the sunshine.

"Get off the porch, Adam, before this destroys you." I tried to tug him into the yard.

"I have to go, Emma. Believe me, we won't be parted forever. We're destined to be together." We both climbed down from the porch. I hurried around to the front, Adam by my side.

"Emma."

I stopped and looked at him, aware of the heat pouring off the wooden house like a bonfire.

"I won't leave you for long. I'll find my way back to you. Wait for me."

He vanished before we reached the street.

I hurried to the sidewalk, driven by burning temperatures and smoke, and pulled my cell phone off my belt. Already I could see fire in every front window, including the attic where smoke was billowing out of the hole the roofer had made in his accident. As the first pane of glass shattered in the heat, I dialed 911. My phone said it was 7:22 p.m.

My second call was to Bev, and she arrived while the siren of the first firetruck could be heard some distance away. Of course, she'd raced out the door and ran the three blocks to where I stood. She didn't scream or sob. Tears silently poured down her face. I don't think she even noticed when it started to rain.

The first firemen on the scene immediately radioed for assistance and managed to keep the fire from spreading to the Fenster-Willoughby house and the smaller house on the other side. I put an arm around Bev as the roof caved in and the rain poured down.

"I loved that house, but it hated me," she whispered.

I gave her a hug.

It was then we heard the howl of pain and anger that seemed to shake the house. It was an unearthly cry, the wail of a fiend descending into hell. What had been unleashed with the fire?

Bev clung to me tighter and let out a sob. I realized I was quaking in fear.

I didn't realize Bobby Aster was there until he walked up to us. Rain pelted his face and slid down his helmet and yellow fire department gear. "Gosh, Emma, Bev, didn't you bring an umbrella?"

"We weren't planning on this, Bobby." Not attempted murder, arson, or ghosts wreaking revenge. No way I'd try to explain that to him or anyone.

"Go home. Get dried off. You're soaked. The fire marshal can get your statements later. And get your neck looked at by a doctor." He stared at the choke marks on my neck. Then, with a hand on each back, he propelled us down the sidewalk.

Bev took three steps and stopped. She turned around and faced him, her voice unnaturally calm. "I suspect it's electrical. The electricians ran into trouble trying to rewire the house, and with those old wires and the workers' power tools, Roger said we were begging for trouble."

Bobby's voice was gentle. "Go home. Get dried off. This can wait. We have it under control."

"The house is gone, isn't it?" I asked.

He nodded. Something in his expression told me this had been a bad day before he got to this fire.

"What's wrong?"

"We had another call first and had trouble getting away from there."

He was a man who cared about people. Something in his tone made me say, "One of your men?"

"Police. He chased a drug pusher on foot. He was shot. The pusher ran into a nearby house that then exploded. Meth lab. The fire spread to the neighboring houses. We had to do multiple rescues."

"How is the policeman?"

"He was still alive when we got him into the ambulance." He shook his head.

I knew most of the cops in the area, many of whom I'd gone to school with. My heart tightened. "Who—?"

"Mike Randall."

He was a sexist jerk, but he was brave and honest and didn't deserve to be murdered any more than Adam had. He was my friend. And Bobby's nephew. My eyes immediately filled with tears and I found it hard to breathe. "Dear Lord. I hope he makes it."

Bobby patted me on the shoulder. "Go home."

"I'm so sorry, Bobby." Then I tugged on Bev. "Let's go to your place and dry you off."

She looked me over and said, "You look like a drowned poodle."

I'd gotten as far as exchanging a sweatshirt borrowed from Bev for my soaked T-shirt and was towel-drying my hair when her doorbell rang. I could hear the shower running, so I ran to answer the door in my bare feet. I didn't recognize the officer in his rain gear standing on the porch. "I was told Miss Winter might be here."

"I'm Emma Winter."

"I'm to take you to the hospital right away."

My heart hit the bottom of my stomach with the weight of a cannonball. "What's happened?"

"Sergeant Randall's been asking for you. You and no one else. The surgeon said we'd find you here."

"Dr. Myers?"

"Yeah."

That part was easily explained. Roger knew Bev and I would be hanging out together. "Surgeons don't usually send policemen to find nonrelatives. What's up?"

"The sergeant demanded to see you and the doctor agreed. I'm to take you over there immediately."

"What aren't you telling me?"

The young patrol officer looked at the polished shoe he was scraping along the porch. "I think you should ask the doctor that."

"He's not here. You are. Speak up." I was worried enough to snap at him.

"Sergeant Randall died once on the operating table. They were able to get him back. Doc's afraid we'll lose him again, since he's been so agitated."

To see me? "Let me tell Bev and get my shoes on."

"You'd better get an umbrella, too."

We rode over using lights and sirens. The young man must have been given strict orders to get me there immediately.

My sneakers made squishing sounds on the tile floors of the hospital corridors and my shorts were clammy against my skin. When we reached the ICU, Roger met me in the entrance to the unit. "It's the damnedest thing. That bullet nicked the carotid artery. Blood poured out of him. We gave him blood but we lost Randall on the operating table. His blood pressure wouldn't come back. Nothing we could do would save him. We pronounced him and pulled all the machines."

He ran a hand through his hair. "Then one of the nurses looks over and yelled for me to come back in. He was breathing on his own. You don't see too many miracles in this business, but this is one of them."

His surprise was still written on his face. "We got him stable and up here, but then he refused to go to sleep, to cooperate, until we brought you in. So here you are. Two minutes, and then you're out."

"Why is he asking for me?"

Roger shrugged. "I have no idea. I don't understand any of this."

"What time did he die?"

He looked at the chart in his hand. "We called it at 7:20. He started breathing again at 7:22."

I went into the unit and was led by a nurse to one of the cubicles. Randall looked very pale, but when he saw me there was a fire in his gorgeous blue eyes I didn't understand.

I took his hand and bent down to hear anything he might say. "It's Emma. I'm here."

His words came out in a cracked whisper. "I told you—believe. We wouldn't—be parted forever."

My heart ricocheted in my chest. "Adam?"

He blinked and smiled.

"I don't understand."

"God has more—to teach me." A smile slid across his face. "Stay—with me, Emma. Please." He stretched one arm with an IV line attached in my direction even as his eyelids were drooping.

I took his hand. "I will. Rest easy."

"Sometime soon, we'll—walk…" There was a pause,

and then his voice faded away as he added, "in—the rain." His hand relaxed, but I wasn't worried. The machines around us all said Mike Randall was alive.

However, I wasn't so sure whose soul was in that bed.

I hope you've enjoyed The Mystery at Chadwick House. This work is available as an ebook on major retailers for sale and free to subscribers of my newsletter. It is also available as a paperback. If you've enjoyed it, please leave me a review on a retailer or on Goodreads. This is my first effort at a contemporary cozy mystery and I'd like to know what you, my readers, think.

Author's notes

The Mystery at Chadwick House was many years in the making. It began at Ghost Walk in New Bern in 2006 or 2007, when while standing in line to tour one of the houses, I was told a story about a modern-day photographer who took a picture of that house and saw a face in an upstairs window. She found the house was empty. When she looked up old photos of the house, she found a match to the face in the window in a 1900 era photograph.

Thirty or forty years ago, I read a story in, I believe, Reader's Digest. Two young women were in a hospital emergency room dying. The young wife and mother, beloved of all, had a brain aneurism burst and was going to die. A young party goer, aimless and out for a good time, had drowned. The staff at the hospital saved the life of the good-time girl at the same time as the young mother expired. The good-time girl turned her life around, studied to become a nurse, and began to attend church. That was where she met the widower of the woman who had died in the hospital bed next to her. They eventually married and she helped raise his children. Every so often, she would say things to the widower that only he and his dead first wife knew. The story had ended with the possibility that the young mother's will to live was so strong that she had taken over the other woman's body so she could see her children grow up and spend more time with her husband.

I combined these two tales and The Mystery at Chadwick House was born.

Talking about my story one day at a neighborhood picnic, one of my neighbors, Bobby Aster, then Fire Chief of New Bern, said he wanted to be in the story. When I finally finished the story, Bobby had now retired from the fire department and had been elected to the Board of Aldermen for the city. Nevertheless, I put Bobby in the story as fire chief and his wife, Jean, as the aunt to my crazy protagonist. They are both terrific, generous people and I hope they like the way I've portrayed them in this story.

I'd like to thank Jen Parker, Hannah Meredith, Ed Hall, and Jennifer Brown for their help in making this story the best it can be.

People who live in and around downtown New Bern have many stories of ghosts residing in the old houses. Some ghosts go back to the Revolutionary War, some to the occupation of New Bern by the Union Army. All are entertaining. If you ever get the chance, visit New Bern, the real-life model for Summerduck, and ask about their ghost stories.

About the Author

Kate Parker caught the reading bug early, and the writing bug soon followed. She's always lived in a home surrounded by books and dust bunnies. After spending twelve years in New Bern, North Carolina, the real-life location for the town in this story, she packed up and moved to Colorado to be closer to family. Now instead of seeing the rivers and beaches of the Atlantic coast, she has the Rocky Mountains for scenery.

Along with The Mystery at Chadwick House, the fourth in the Deadly series, Deadly Deception, will be coming out this spring. She's already at work on the next Milliner Mystery while researching the fifth in the Deadly series. She reports she is having fun creating new stories to entertain readers and chaos to challenge her characters.

Follow Kate and her deadly examination of history at www.KateParkerbooks.com
and www.Facebook.com/Author.Kate.Parker/